THE STAR OF ATLANTIS

THE STAR OF ATLANTIS SERIES
BOOK 2

TRICIA D. WAGNER

LYRIDAE BOOKS

DEDICATION

I often find myself astonished to have tasted the exhilaration and wonder that is writing. I sometimes feel I've slipped inside the mountain of the gods and stolen their secret fire.

This book is for Brian, whose steadfastness has helped me believe that I can learn the art of wielding flames.

- Tricia D. Wagner

PRAISE FOR TRICIA D. WAGNER

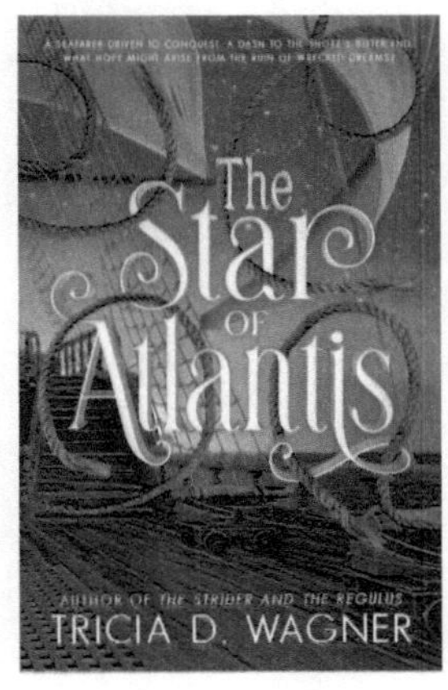

"The blend of intrigue, supernatural influences, and the dilemma faced by Swift as he tries to save his brother Caius highlights a journey far from home that might never bring him back. Wagner does a particularly fine job of portraying shifting friendships as Swift comes to find that his friendship with Ash is changed by the Star of Atlantis. These underlying probes of the impact of an adventure add a dimension of psychological introspection to the story that places it more than a notch above the usual action story."

-D. Donovan, Sr. Reviewer, *Midwest Book Review*

We must free ourselves of the hope that the sea will ever rest.
We must learn to sail in high winds.

\- Aristotle Onassis

1

FIVE YEARS AGO

*E*ight-year-old Swift pointed the tip of his rapier straight at his best friend's face. "Surrender, or you'll wear the mark of my blade on your mug for the whole ship to laugh at."

"Never!" said Swift's best friend, Ash—already bearing three marks on his face, inflicted with red ink. He swiped the blade aside with his own rapier (duller than Swift's, not as jeweled). "You give up, or I'll leave you with a pretty good scar for scaring the ladies."

"Swift," Mum called. "Off the dock, please. If you and Ash want to play at invisible swords, come do it by the house. Let's have no spills into the water."

"I don't care a heap of sardines for the ladies." Swift lunged.

A tap with a finger meant a rapier strike and entitled the aggressor to scrawl a mark on the victim.

Swift did. Right across Ash's cheek. It looked real. Bloody.

Ash, clutching his chest, sunk to his knees. "This wound's mortal!"

"No it isn't." Swift backed up. "I just clipped your cheek."

"Well, say that you didn't." Ash got to his feet. "Say you plunged it home in my chest or belly. Say you did. That'd be a mortal wound and much more interesting."

"All right." Swift took his stance and thrust the rapier straight to the chest.

Home went the blade. Ash sprawled on the dock and dropped into a fit of theatrical twitching.

"Come off the dock, lads," yelled Caius, Swift's best older brother.

Mum followed Caius up the path leading to the beach house. "Now!"

"Be right there." Swift, holding his marker cocked, knelt over Ash. "I just have to finish off this pirate rascal."

"Make it quick," came Mum's irritated voice, from the beach house's doorway.

Swift applied a line of red jagged ink across Ash's chest, at the left intercostal space where Caius had taught him the heart beats the strongest.

One mighty last twitch—and...

Ash was gone.

Dead as a driftwood plank.

Ash raised himself to his elbows. "Bet you can't get me again."

Swift glanced toward the beach house.

Mum and Caius weren't there. Neither was his father. They all must've gone inside.

They wanted Swift and Ash up by the house, but—invisible swords was far better played with a backdrop of water.

Swift narrowed his eyes at Ash. "Bet I can."

And he certainly could. In a meeting of rapiers, Swift almost always prevailed. It was about the only thing at which Ash ever allowed Swift to win, making each victory honey sweet.

Ash was way more competitive, better in every sport, and friends with everyone. And he made sure Swift knew it.

"Your blade won't so much as come near me," Ash said with gusto. "But look how mine bites!" He rushed Swift.

Swift eased aside, sending Ash tumbling to his knees on the dock. "Yours bites, does it? Seems tame as a tuna fish to me."

Ash clambered to his feet and ran at Swift.

A smart flick did the job, and Ash stumbled once again, gripping his ribs where a rapier handle would be sticking out.

Sometimes it felt like this game of swordplay—Ash perpetually losing—was his attempt to keep Swift, tiring of always trailing behind, from shaking him off.

Swift could best Ash in any subject at school, though. People called Swift a savant at languages—he'd grown fluent in French, German, and Welsh early, his father and mum presenting them to him along with English as a baby.

And since starting school, he'd picked up Italian and Greek. He absorbed new languages so quickly that his older brothers—Caius, Trystan, and Edric—regularly entertained themselves by giving him characters and words from dead languages to play with—to watch Swift, right before their eyes, sop them up.

He had about a thousand Egyptian hieroglyphs and hieroglyphic word groupings memorized. He knew Latin and Sicilian and Karaim well enough to read whole books written in them. And in Celtic Akkadian, he could fluidly translate both ways.

As strong as he was at his languages, though, he was yet stronger in maths. In mathematics, Swift was a match to first-year college students, and he was now even learning from the same textbook Caius was using in his maths for medicine class.

In academics, he could truly best anyone. But on that score, Ash refused to compete.

"I'm finished," Ash whispered. "You're witness to the last words of Captain Ash, Pirate Tormentor of the Cold Celtic Sea."

Swift saluted.

Ash spun on a heel and fell backwards.

A glorious, tragic fall it would've been, had his aim had been on point toward the dock. But he fell right off its edge and splashed into the water.

Swift rushed to the dock's edge.

Ten feet down sloshed an indigo blue, restless sea, steadily breaking itself on the shore rocks.

"Ash?"

Nothing.

He waited.

If this were a trick, Ash would have to come up in a second.

"Ash?"

Bubbles. Some rippling. And then—steady waves.

Ash wasn't coming up.

Ash was drowning.

"Mum!" cried Swift. "Father!"

No one came out of the house.

Swift started to run to it but stopped. He stared at the dark, rocking water. Ash was down there.

He crashed to his knees on the dock.

He'd been trained to help struggling swimmers. Well, not trained, exactly, but he'd seen it. Well, not directly, but online. And Caius had done it and told him about it.

"Mum," he screamed. "Father! Caius!"

He could dive, but—Caius once told him that in water accidents, the rescuer often drowns, too.

Kneeling on the dock before the rough waves, Swift could comprehend why.

The water was turbulent and deep here, where the dock met the shore rocks. Plus, it was cold. Ice cold.

Swift looked back toward the beach house.

There was no one in sight.

No one was coming.

He stripped off his trousers and kicked off his shoes. He filled his lungs with possibly all the coastal air in Wales. Then he dove.

Down he sank, his body convulsing with the agony of cold water. Down to where the light thinned. Down into worlds removed from air. Down toward where a pale hand drifted beside a dark head.

The burning in Swift's lungs started well above where Ash hung. Swift had to let go of bubbles, precious oxygen bubbles to keep his diaphragm from sucking down seawater.

His eyes stinging, his heartbeat deafening, Swift struggled down, down to the eerie weeds swaying on the seafloor.

He caught Ash's hand and dragged him up from the murk.

Holding Ash's limp body to his chest, he kicked.

He let out more bubbles.

Broke the water's surface.

He drew a deep breath while shadows cleared from his eyes.

Ash didn't breathe.

His eyes weren't open.

"Ash." Swift kicked toward the shore rocks.

But the current was a fist dragging them out to sea.

Already, they were a dozen feet from the shore, and the breakers weren't giving him any chance to reach it.

Don't panic, he thought. Float. Keep parallel to the coast. Don't try to swim to it—that's a losing fight.

Swift breathed as steadily as he could between the waves. He kicked, keeping parallel to the coast.

He glanced around for anything to grab onto, but there was nothing. Ash's cold body, rubbery, was the only thing nearby to grip, and as strongly as Swift was trying to keep them both afloat, it seemed to be dragging him down.

He struggled to think.

Swim parallel to the coast. That's all he knew about surviving a fall into the sea. He'd many times, on his father's ship, imagined falling overboard. But he'd never imagined doing it with his best friend—not breathing—in tow.

A tall wave splashed over them, dousing their faces.

Swift heaved Ash higher, resting the back of his head against on his own shoulder.

Ash coughed up water. Breathed. Cried out.

Arms grasping. Legs kicking.

Swift could barely keep hold of him.

"Ash, stop." He managed a tighter grip. "Calm down. I have you. Keep breathing."

"Who has you?" Ash rasped.

Swift thought fast. "The kraken. Its tentacles are holding us up."

Ash seemed to be picturing it. He let off with trying to wrap his arms around Swift's head.

"Don't move, okay? Not a muscle. Trust me."

"I want my father." Ash was crying. "You let me fall. Why'd you let me fall in?"

The water spun them away from the rocky shore and carried them north of the beach house.

Swift had been in water this cold before, but never without a wetsuit. After just these few minutes, his legs were tending numb.

Mum came into view. "Swift?" She scanned the dock, the edge of the shore rocks. "Ash?"

"Mum," Swift shouted.

'Help' would've been next, but he swallowed a mouthful of water.

Mum screamed.

She raced over a stretch of sandy land to the rocky sea wall.

Running along the waterline, she seemed faster than the current, but barely. And by the time she reached the end of the shore rocks, the water was spinning Swift and Ash toward the open ocean.

The open ocean. Where jellyfish and conger eels drifted. Where sharks swam.

Swift couldn't control his breathing going manic.

He twisted to facing the coast. He stared at Mum—running along the shore and not keeping up.

"Let go," said Ash. "I can swim."

Ash probably couldn't swim, or not well, after what'd happened to him. And apart, the current might carry them each faster. Or him this way and Ash that.

Mum might be able to reach one of them, but not both.

They had to stay together.

Water smashed into them.

"Let go of me." Ash squirmed.

A wave buried them.

Up they came, Swift gripping Ash's shoulders with arms he couldn't feel.

Ash fought to get away. Clawed Swift's arms. Kicked. Swiped at his face.

Even if he'd wanted to, though, Swift couldn't have let go of him. His arms were frozen, contracted around Ash's shoulders—they wouldn't unbend.

"You're killing me," said Ash.

Swift kicked as hard as he could to stay over the waves. "Hey—what's that?"

Ash stilled.

"In the sky," said Swift. "There. What is that?"

"Where?"

The current twisted them to face the open ocean.

"The clouds," said Swift. "Look at those clouds."

"There aren't any clouds."

"One coming from the north is shaped just like a pirate ship. See it?"

"Where?"

Heavy hands gripped them and cast them onto a body board.

"Hang on, lads, tight as you can." It was Swift's father. Justus.

He saw their hands fixed on the board, then kicked hard, ferrying them to the shore.

2

THIS MORNING

Swift gripped the mast of his dinghy, the *Star Strider*, and braced for the enormous wave advancing.

Edric, his oldest brother, reached to tighten the sail.

"Don't. I can do it," Swift hollered.

They barreled over the wave, toward the rough waters churning through the mouth of a large cove.

This cove lay nestled farther north along the Pembrokeshire coast than Swift had ever sailed. Inside the curve of its pock-marked sea wall, he could truly imagine the Star of Atlantis— the most renowned lost sea relic in Wales—lying hidden.

"You've lost control of our heading," said Edric.

Swift cast him a look. He was in total control.

"Ropes tight," called Edric. "Keep the ropes tight."

"I know what I'm doing."

And he certainly did. He already knew how to navigate by reading the stars (which Edric couldn't do), and he'd learned the trails of currents winding through this Celtic Sea.

He'd also memorized the temper of the winds and waves in all seasons, and now he'd acquired a whole weekend of actual sailing practice, and he'd come on by leaps and bounds.

This cove was the third, the largest, and the roughest that Swift had explored in the *Strider* since dawn.

In the first two, Swift had done well—even their father, Justus, had said so.

But the first two coves had held easy waters that the *Strider* could cut right through. Swift scarcely even needed to manage the wind, the tug of smooth coastal currents ferrying them along like children in a wagon.

When Justus assessed this cove, he'd waffled about whether Swift and Edric ought to even try it. The forecasters had predicted a chance of storms moving in over the next several hours.

But Justus ended by calling the cove's temper "lightly fussy, but manageable," and "a good challenge for the lad."

Now that he was all the way in the drink of these breakers, Swift recognized what it meant for sailors to talk of "a beast of a sea." The sharper waves cast up the *Strider* in spasms, creating a pitch and roll so fierce that Swift and Edric were having to keep their feet jammed to her corners to hold her upright.

And there was a smell of death on the wind, some carcass hauled here by the white rushing waters.

"Straighten out our heading, or I'm taking over," said Edric.

"I've got it." Swift yanked the rope of the *Strider's* mast.

Edric yelled, "Tighter!"

Swift rushed the *Strider* toward two tall waves and angled the craft between them, its slide smooth. Perfect.

Swift met Edric's glare. "I told you I had it."

"Keep your eyes on what's coming."

Swift had protested when Justus determined that each of Swift's older brothers would disembark his big ship, the *Regulus Borealis*, and take a turn piloting the dinghy with Swift. But Justus wouldn't be moved. After what Swift pulled in the night —taking the *Strider* out to sea on his own—he was lucky to be sailing this morning at all.

But at thirteen, relying on his brothers to look after him in any form struck as mortifying.

Caius had been happy to sail in the dinghy with Swift, and of course they'd had fun. Trystan had been agreeable enough, but he'd taken their cove quickly, and his interest felt faked.

Edric had rolled his eyes, demanded the last shift, and settled in the stern of the *Regulus* until his number came up.

Each cove had been interesting in its own way, but in none of them had Swift found any hint of the Star of Atlantis.

But of the three coves Swift had chosen, this one seemed the most optimal for hidden treasure to rest.

This cove's edges and islets were cratered with tide pools, like a meteor-marred old moon. The long-lost treasure might've drifted into one of them.

Granted, the biggest islet, in the center of this cove, didn't look all that similar to the "round as Earth" islet described on his *Star of Atlantis* map, in his *Star of Atlantis* book. But this islet's edges did somewhat curve.

Edric took Swift by the shoulders. "You missed a buckle on your lifejacket."

Swift jerked away. "Don't pull me like that. I can't hold the ropes with you twisting me."

"Hand over those ropes and tend to your lifejacket." Edric yanked the ropes out of Swift's hands.

Swift glared at him.

"You think I give a damn if you're mad?" asked Edric. "Latch that jacket tight. Now."

Swift fastened the buckle. "Can I have the ropes back?"

"I'd think you'd have learned to be more cautious after the Tumble." Edric smirked.

Swift snatched back the ropes.

The Tumble hadn't happened because Swift had failed to be cautious. In truth, it wasn't even he who'd "tumbled." It'd been Ash.

But no one ever thought about it like that. They cheerfully called it "the Tumble" because that was easier on the heart than calling it "the near death."

"I didn't do anything wrong that day," said Swift. "I don't care who says it was my fault."

Although, in a way, it had been his fault. He hadn't come away from the dock when Mum asked him to.

"I didn't say it was your fault," said Edric.

"But you were thinking it," said Swift. "You're always thinking it. Justus thinks it was, too."

"He does not. And I just like teasing you about it."

Edric more than "liked" teasing Swift. Edric had refined picking on his youngest brother to a science.

Swift glanced at the sun. It was already past noon. But they still might have a couple of hours before any storm would roll in.

"Can we focus on sailing?" Swift adjusted the rope. "Let's just make it to the coast or that islet."

"It's you who's been slack on our heading. Decide where you want to make landfall."

Swift studied that biggest islet and gauged the turbulent water dividing them from it.

"Watch it!" hollered Edric.

Two waves collided in front of the *Strider*—two Norse giants locked in a battle of wills—their conflict resolving in the destruction of them both, their shapes compounding in a tower of water that burst over the *Strider*.

Swift stiffened at the soaking.

His sailing suit would dry quick and keep him somewhat warm—but freshly drenched by water this cold, every sailor would feel his breath hitching.

Swift shook off the bite and tightened the sail.

Edric tossed water out of his hair. "See, you ought to be glad you have brothers who'll make sure your lifejacket's sound."

Swift yanked the sail's rope. He didn't need brothers to help him manage his lifejacket.

His whole family had gone obsessive about lifejackets, though, after the Tumble, and the tic had taken hold. They were all still neurotic, even though it'd happened five long years ago.

"You're flagging." Edric tightened Swift's hands on the ropes. "If you don't want us bashed on those rocks, you'll have to keep the ropes firm."

A flash of sapphire water rolled at them from the open ocean.

Swift gripped the mast and held his breath, readying for a buck.

His ankles, against the sides of the dinghy, burned.

But as the wave passed, the *Strider* slid up it and perched on a swell's round peak. Swift coasted her into a series of smooth troughs, sea spray spattering him.

They'd made it through the roughest breakers and were drifting now into the center of the cove, surveying it from a gentler plane.

Water dripping off the curls before Swift's eyes sheened the cove with afternoon light. A salty white sun sailed along at a quick clip on the backs of windswept clouds.

Though these waves were gentler, the water was tending shallow, and reefs stood out of the sea here and there.

Edric shoved Swift aside and managed the sail until they were skidding away from a boulder, then coasting back to the clearer water drawing toward the big islet.

"Sit behind me," said Edric. "Take the rudder. I'll have the sail from here."

"These are easier waters. I can—"

"I said move."

Swift slipped back and settled in the rear of the dinghy while Edric took the center bench.

Swift glanced back through the cove's mouth toward the *Regulus*, holding Caius, Trystan, and Justus. They were minuscule, barely visible, watching from the deck.

Seeing them all there, all with him, chasing his treasure—it soothed the wound Ash had laid yesterday, crowing over Swift about how often his own father took him sailing.

Soon after the Tumble, Ash had cornered Swift in the woods between their houses. Swift had let the accident happen, Ash said. Swift was a bad person and a terrible friend. Ash had almost died, and it was Swift's fault.

Ash brought with him all the pirate toys Swift had left at his house and all the play treasure he'd won. He dumped everything in the dirt at Swift's feet.

What Ash had not returned were Swift's rare maritime books—dozens of them—collected over years. No matter how Swift asked, Ash refused to give them back.

And he swore to everyone that he didn't have them; that Swift's accusation was a lie.

Since they'd parted ways, Ash had plunged into sea legends as arduously as Swift had.

And earlier this year, Ash discovered a real lead on an alleged treasure chest that, legend had it, was stowed in some coastal cave in the north of Pembrokeshire.

Ash's theory, drawn together using information from Swift's rare books, had won him a feature in the school paper, with his picture and everything.

Though it made Swift sick to look at that article, he'd kept it. Ash's research on the location of that treasure chest wasn't bad, and it was the only access he had now to those insights.

What Ash didn't have, though, what Swift had managed to keep, was his most precious book—*The Star of Atlantis*. It held insights into the most renowned mythical treasure in Wales.

"Well don't just sit there, point out our heading," called Edric.

Swift studied the big islet for a landing site.

Stretches of rocks stood out of the sea like gothic spires, making the way to the islet seem impossible. And rough waves were lashing its edges.

But a trail of water stretching to the islet's northern rim looked clear enough of the outcrops.

Even the current pulling that way seemed a touch less petulant.

"The northern side of the big islet." Swift pointed. "Do you see those crevices that seem perfect for treasure concealing?"

"I have to shoot straight with you." Edric glanced back at him. "You're not going to find any Star of Atlantis in those crags. Or anyplace."

"The Star of Atlantis could very well rest there—it's never been found." Swift aimed the *Strider's* rudder to guide them toward the northern side of the islet. "And I bet Ash hasn't got the guts to go sailing anyplace like this."

"The Star of Atlantis, whatever it is, has to be more legend than real," said Edric.

"There are too many accounts of it, historically, to write it off as legend," said Swift. "Odds are—it does exist."

"And do any of those accounts say what it is?"

Swift's book didn't say what the Star of Atlantis was, but that seemed not to matter.

What it did say, was—

When the shore draws long and straight, skim the briny banks.
Be swallowed by Sterncastle Cove. Seek the islet, round as
Earth...

These instructions, written both in his *Star of Atlantis* book and on its map—cryptic as they were—did sort of describe the coastline leading up to this cove.

Edric raised his brows at Swift's silence. "So, you have no idea what it is, much less where?"

Swift glanced off.

"Right," said Edric.

Swift had admitted to himself hours ago that he had very little chance of happening upon the right cove today, having done almost no research.

They were skimming the coastline edging the Wentletrap Forest, and the map was crystal clear that the treasure was stowed near the Wentletrap.

But there were indeed dozens upon dozens of coves along this stretch of Pembrokeshire.

Despite that he could imagine finding the Star of Atlantis here—truth be told, he was feeling some shame for bringing his father and brothers all the way out here for nothing.

His drive for keeping at treasure hunting today was honestly based on a foolish hope that they'd just get lucky. That he'd find something interesting that would insulate him from the criticism that this venture had amounted to zilch.

"Your book, along with that map you found," said Edric, "they're fantasies. Right?"

"They're historical," said Swift. "They do tell its location—roughly—which is all that I need. If I can get to the right cove, to the right islet, I'll find out what the Star of Atlantis is. There's nothing wrong with that logic."

"You don't care that you haven't a clue what you're looking for? If the Star of Atlantis does exist, it might just be rubbish. Maybe something sentimental to whoever hid it, but worthless today."

"Or, it might be priceless," said Swift.

"No matter what it is—or was—you have to admit that it'll never turn up. If it ever existed, it'd have to be rotting in some trench by now."

"Or," said Swift, "it could be in one of those crevices."

Edric studied the water, growing calm. He let the sail be. "Answer me this, Little Brother. How does a lad as sharp as you grow obsessed with something as fickle as legends of treasure?"

Fickle.

Swift sat taller. "Wasn't it you who said to me, just this morning, that growing up is about finding your own way? Didn't you even say that you thought I was like you?"

"The call of a different drum seems to speak to both of us," said Edric. "But—don't you think that going after some lost, probably fictional, relic, which no one can even describe, is sinking to Ash's level a little?"

"If he'd given me back my books, I'd have the Star of Atlantis—or something, by now."

"The odds of you finding anything are terribly low, right? So why pretend otherwise?"

Swift shrugged. "I'm thirteen, and—"

"Don't give me that. You're smarter than, 'I'm thirteen.'"

"Okay, then I'm also smart enough to pay attention to what others might disregard."

"That isn't it," said Edric. "The truth is—you're lost."

Swift jerked the rudder to angle the *Strider* truer to the big islet.

"And you've been lost for some time," said Edric. "Ever since the Tumble, you've seemed not to trust yourself. Last night, when you filched the *Strider*—that was the first time in years that I've seen real confidence in you."

Swift focused on the rudder.

"And last night, when Justus caught you," said Edric, "did he not tell you exactly what he wants from you?"

Justus wanted Swift to buckle down with his studies hard enough to finish school early and test into a Practicum for fifteen-year-old students prepping to read medicine. Justus talked of wanting Swift to "take risks," "invest himself," and "learn the meaning of sacrifice."

"You don't think you're capable of delivering what he wants, do you?" asked Edric.

Swift glanced at Edric's eyes, wide and impatient for a response.

Edric asked, "Do you even want to try for that Practicum?"

It wasn't that Swift didn't like the thought of trying for it. Caius was years into medical school, and the trauma medicine he studied was endlessly cool.

But the idea of discarding what Edric called "an obsession" (which was actually love) for sea venturing, for chasing the unknown and hunting treasure—it felt like a self-betrayal.

And anyway, after the Tumble, Swift couldn't help but put together that "risking," "investing," and "sacrificing" to try to rescue someone had ended with Ash hating him. If Swift followed where Justus was leading, who else might cast him off?

"Am I right?" asked Edric. "Are you lost?"

From the line of white water flashing against the big islet, a flock of seagulls took to the wing, swirling in an uptick of wind.

The wind strengthened the potency of the rotten flesh smell.

Something had died in the water, just past that islet. Something big.

A spectacular carcass must be floating over there, concealed by the islet's higher rocks.

Swift let his gaze rest on the soaring birds, diving to pick clean the body of the thing.

A carcass was no treasure, but it would be an unforgettable sight. Even Edric might think it was cool. At any rate, it would be more worthwhile to discover than nothing at all.

Swift set the rudder to move the *Strider* toward the commotion.

"What—are you afraid of the answer?" asked Edric.

Swift kept his gaze low.

The Practicum was so selective that all but one or two students failed. How could anyone not feel lost, facing that?

"Are you afraid you can't handle what Justus is offering?" asked Edric.

"I know I can't handle it." The words were out before Swift could think.

This was one of the worst things about Edric. He was good at manipulation and could get what he wanted out of anyone— even Swift, who could see what he was doing.

"But here's the thing." Edric leaned in. "You can handle it. You're just afraid to be tested."

Swift grew hot, some out of frustration. More because Edric was right.

Edric smirked. "You're easy to read, Little Brother."

"Why are you saying all this to me?" Swift gripped the rudder, stuttering the boat. "You want me to face his plan, don't you? You think I'll fail, and you just want to watch."

Edric glanced around. "I can see exactly what you're doing with all this pirate lore obsession and treasure rubbish, too."

Swift cast his gaze toward the water. "I'm not 'doing' anything."

"You want to prove yourself to Justus, here, on the strong North Atlantic, so you'll feel justified when you finally work up the nerve to tell him you won't be what he wants. He gave you the perfect chance last night to shoot straight with him and say 'no.' But you didn't. You strung him along."

"And what if I do want to try for the Practicum?" Swift glanced up. "I mean, I'm not saying I do, but—what if?"

"Look, if you go after that Practicum, you'll have to be absolutely obsessed—even more so than you are with the Star of Atlantis. And you'll have to go at it for your own reasons. If you do it only to win Justus' respect, you're certainly going to fail."

"I do want his respect." The words came out harder than Swift meant them to.

Edric was prying him open too wide. Swift bit his lip to keep anything else from slipping out.

He wished he could trust Edric, that he could talk openly about this with him. Edric was right that both of them heard the call of a different drum.

But growing up with Edric and his cynicism, his temper—Swift had learned to keep his guard high.

Edric gazed about the cove. "So all this venturing—is it about impressing Justus?"

"I don't know." Swift again bit his lip.

Edric gestured to the dinghy's bench as he moved off it. "If that's your game, then have the mainsail. Take your bench."

Swift had no choice but to take it. He had to move with Edric to keep the *Strider* balanced.

He eased onto the center bench and adjusted the mainsail—way better than how Edric had set it. He caught a brisk wind that cruised them toward the wheeling gulls.

Edric unhooked an oar and steadied the *Strider* when rough sloshing set them off course. "I don't want to see you fail, you know."

Swift didn't dignify that with any response. It would take more than Edric making the claim for Swift to believe it.

"Swift, ahead!" shouted Edric.

Out of nowhere—reefs Swift hadn't marked, rose from a trough.

Swift angled the sail into a wind that carried the *Strider* keenly through a narrow pass between the two clusters of rocks.

He tossed Edric a glance. "Think that'd impress Justus?"

"Don't get cocky. Watch where you're taking us."

Swift broadened the sail and navigated back to clear water.

The *Strider* was now coasting near enough to the islet to glimpse the carcass—unidentifiable and huge—a humpish brain-gray mass, bloated and stark beneath the ashen shadows of circling birds.

It wasn't difficult to imagine that so much necrotic flesh might be the decaying tentacles of a great Kraken, slain.

Krakens were fictional, like most purported treasure, of course. But who knew?

Maybe Krakens did wander the deeps. Maybe this was one. The ocean was full of all manner of mysteries.

The dead thing bobbed in lifts of water but wasn't moving high enough for Swift to see any detail.

Edric jabbed him. "You're wondering if that's a kraken, aren't you? You and that imagination."

"That" imagination. The Tumble. Justus' daunting plan. Swift's "obsession" with sea lore and lost pirate treasure.

Edric was needling at Swift's most tender parts. Is this why he'd agreed to sail with him—just to score a cheap rise?

Swift maneuvered the *Strider* through surges, strategizing a wide approach to the dead thing, and set the sail for it.

But the waves wouldn't have it. Swift lost most of the distance on every meter he gained.

"Want me to take over?" asked Edric, a satisfied smirk on his face.

"*Come hell,*" Swift whispered, quoting the seafarer's oath in *The Star of Atlantis*. "*Come storm waters. Come the Kraken.*"

His father's call to dream, not of treasure, but of adulthood —of gearing up to read medicine—it seemed not just daunting, but so abstract, tangential to the wonderful fury and muscle burn of this present fight.

Life couldn't be just about planning. Life couldn't be a vague hour, years from now, when he'd leave for some university. Real life, it seemed, was this moment.

"*I'll forsake all sound shores for the night-lighted passage-ways—untrodden reaches—for sun-brightened visions, for insights of stars.*" Swift sped them down a slick wave, his stomach leaping in the rush.

And then a back current from the big islet's shore heaved them sideways.

Swift spilled off the bench, into the *Strider's* bowl.

The little boat tipped.

Edric grabbed the mast and rocked her into balance.

Swift pulled to the bench and looked down at a sharp stinging on his arm.

His windbreaker was torn, sliced by a sharp-edged screw on the dinghy's rail.

Beneath the ripped fabric, dark blood welled.

"Lord, what'd you do?" Edric guided the dinghy clear of a reef, then sat before Swift.

He drew back Swift's sleeve.

The inside of Swift's forearm was marred with a cut a good three inches long. Blood was slipping out it quick, pooling inside his jacket.

Swift's vision blotched at the sight.

"Looks like medicine isn't the only venture that requires a strong stomach," said Edric.

Swift tried to take over the ropes.

"I'll sail. You just hang in." Edric kept him fixed on the bench, his head down.

Swift spread his sliced jacket and made himself study the cut and its blood.

The cut was deep, though not the worst injury he'd ever suffered. That'd been once when he stepped on a nail. He'd all but passed out at the sight of metal sticking out of a bloody hole in his body, and he'd heaved when Caius pulled it out.

Swift held his breath, swallowing down nausea. He snugged his sleeve tight around his arm. He snatched a spare bit of nylon rope and wound it around his sleeve, pulling it taut with his teeth.

He held steady for a minute, letting the cold wind dry the sweat on his face.

When he felt a good distance from the brink of passing out, he glanced around.

Edric was advancing in open water toward a tiny islet, far removed from the one they'd been trying to reach.

"Don't bank us." Swift picked up the oar. "We'll never get back out."

Edric yanked the oar from him. "I'm calling it."

A current swirling near the small islet snatched the *Strider* and sent her cruising toward it.

The sea shoved, the hull's bottom scraped, and the *Strider* was aground on the islet's slate ledge.

Swift waited a moment, feeling for the swell of the sea to lift the craft, to pull her back out. But when the water sucked the rocks, the *Strider* didn't move.

They were hard grounded, and the surges striking the islet were strong. They certainly wouldn't make it back onto the water, even if they wanted to.

Swift glanced at the sun and calculated how long until the tide would rise, burying these rocks and giving lift to the *Strider*.

The tide wouldn't flow again for more than three hours. And if storms were on the way, they'd hit before then.

Swift glanced at his torn wrist; glanced at the *Regulus*, lowing in the distance.

3

Swift studied the rocks they'd washed up on.

The sea was gushing across their crags, but in a shallow enough way to make the inner boulders passable by foot.

Edric unwound the *Strider's* tow rope and stepped over the gunwale. Swift followed him out and steadied himself near the center of the islet.

The islet's pinnacles were high enough that they seemed barely splashed by the waves. And the water wasn't more than ankle deep over most of the surface. The lower pools made basins holding crystal-clear ocean and bright tidal stones.

There, colorful plants swayed in gentle underwater winds. Sky-blue and tangerine starfish, gazing from their pools, clung to walls knobby with barnacles and anemones.

Blood ran from Swift's hand and dripped off his fingertip into a pool.

"You stay put there." Edric moved to the islet's edge and hauled the *Strider* into a crevasse between two rocks. He set to lashing the *Strider's* rope to a boulder.

Swift crouched in the shallow water, steadying himself against a burst of wind. He rolled back his sleeve.

Blood seeped from the cut.

He cradled his arm, holding it to his chest as tightly as he could tolerate.

Something on a boulder beside him slipped off and splashed into a tide pool.

"What the—"

Swift dipped his uninjured hand into the water. He drew it out and opened his palm to discover a wriggling baby octopus.

"Whoa."

He'd never held an octopus. He'd never even seen a picture of one so black-as-night, pricked with tiny electric blue stars.

The octopus squiggled its eight stretchy tentacles onto Swift's knee.

"Are you a spawn of a kraken?" He set it on his windbreaker and guided it to crawl up him.

This was no Star of Atlantis, but it was so cool.

Swift glanced at Edric, trying to catch his eye. Maybe, seeing this, Edric would call their venture worthwhile.

"Don't mess with that," said Edric. "Help me light a rocket flare."

Swift held up the octopus. "How can you not think this is extraordinary? Look at her!"

He watched the tiny sea creature coil its arms into ebony rings.

"She's just letting me hold her."

Edric held out a flare. "I'd like to see you do the lighting."

Swift perched the octopus on his elbow as he made his way to Edric. "We'll have to broadcast our distress," he told what seemed to be the octopus' face.

Edric rolled his eyes. "Will you get on with it?"

Early this morning, Edric had claimed that he saw some of himself in Swift.

That admission had been a true shock. But it'd felt good.

In moments like this, though, (and more moments were like this than not), Edric seemed to have no tolerance for Swift—and he seemed even to dislike him.

Edric's fed-up expression incited a pain in the chest—like a heart's chamber had gone cold, icy sea water dribbling in and dousing an ember.

This wasn't a new pain, though. It was the sort of pain you feel when people see you with no guard; when they realize the person that they hoped to find doesn't match who you really are. When they discover they're disappointed in you.

Swift, doing his best to avoid meeting Edric's wide eyes, took the flare. He coaxed the octopus to creep onto his chest. He set the rocket flare's trigger and fired it.

The flare erupted, spitting red sparks in a tight spiral fifty feet up. It coasted, a burning red shimmer, over their islet.

In the distance, the *Regulus* roused, its handsome sails broadening.

Though moving at a steady clip, the ship's advance would be a crawl. Even with the engine fired, their father's great brigantine wasn't fast.

Edric settled onto the edge of the islet and pulled Swift to sitting beside him. He eased up Swift's sleeve.

Swift couldn't look any more at the blood. Instead, he stared at his feet, clad in blue water shoes, plunked in the sea.

Beneath them, the waves were clear, but darkly so. He studied the depths for motion, for anything that might be rising.

It felt vulnerable to sit here, and not just because islets could be precarious with high waves smashing in out of nowhere. Sharks trolled these waters in dense concentrations, hunting for carrion washed in by the turbulent currents.

If a shark were looming in this fearful abyss, drawn by the carcass the shorebirds were tearing, would Swift even be able to see it?

When he'd seen the thrasher shark early this morning, from within the *Strider*, he'd had no clue that a shark was anyplace close until it was cutting the water and airborne.

A delicious fear unfurled inside him, sending an electric sensitivity into his hands and feet.

He forced his feet to stay down in the water until his toes were positively screaming with instinctual terror to jerk out and scatter back.

He focused on wanting, desperately, to see a shark. But he didn't want to see a shark! He waited for a shark.

Something brushed his ankle.

Swift jerked up his legs and held them at the surface.

A frond of seaweed bubbled up.

Edric righted him. "Can't you ever be still?" Finishing his look at the cut, he held his hand tight over it.

The pain of it made Swift's vision go gray.

The cut felt not just tender, like a scratch, but bruised. The agony of it—a dull throb, made Swift wonder if the screw had torn into some muscle. Even with the pressure of Edric's hand on it, blood was welling.

Edric shook him. "Hey, are you blacking out?"

"No." Swift sat straighter. He focused on the seascape—the coves and the blueness of the water carrying the *Regulus* to them.

But he couldn't focus on the waves long. They seemed to be making the dizziness worse.

He studied his gray waterproof sailing trousers, his skinny ankles peeking from them.

His skin looked a dead, washed-out blue in the swelling sea's top.

It was troubling to see the ghostly impression of flesh underwater. When he'd first sighted Ash's hand floating up from the deeps, he really thought Ash had died.

Edric, watching him, seemed to be reading him. "You've come an awfully long way, handling the sea as you do. Not many people who've faced nearly drowning would take to the water so well."

This mixture of interest and callousness coming from Edric was confounding. Swift eased away from him. "I've never been afraid of the sea."

The North Atlantic was like a wild animal that'd bitten him. But for that he didn't resent it. Could a wild thing be blamed for its wildness? If anything, by the Tumble, Swift understood the sea better.

What he couldn't understand was Ash.

When they ran into each other, even now, five years later, it was like Ash couldn't tolerate Swift any better than Edric could.

Or he'd bully Swift into some mad competition that Swift was bound to lose. Ash certainly had stolen his books, and not because he really loved seafaring or Norse pirate lore. The truth was, he loathed the idea of Swift gaining any edge.

"I didn't do anything wrong," whispered Swift to himself, to the octopus, seeming wholly at peace on his knee.

Though the deadly sea didn't daunt Swift, Ash's criticism, his manipulations certainly did. Anytime Ash maneuvered him into competing—anytime he challenged or threatened him— Swift panicked.

The only relief came from the notion of eventually getting the better of Ash. Or learning to wholly ignore him. Both seemed impossible.

"I've told you, forget Ash," said Edric. "I know how that lad thinks, and I promise you, he's not worth worrying over. And besides, without you, he'd be dead."

"Well to him, I'm dead," said Swift. "He still hates me. If I never saw him again, I wouldn't care. Even as much as I avoid him, though, he's always getting in my way."

"Good God." Edric eased up on Swift's arm. He gazed off at the *Regulus*.

"What?"

"I see it now." Edric turned his gaze onto Swift. "That's your whole problem."

Swift shrugged. "What are you talking about?"

Edric tightened his hand again on Swift's arm. "You're a runner."

Swift winced.

"You run from what you can't deal with," said Edric.

"No. I don't."

"Ah, so, you haven't been avoiding Ash? You haven't been dodging Justus these last months?"

Swift used his free hand to lift the baby octopus and dip her in a tide pool.

In the cold crystal water, she still didn't leave him. She unfurled her tentacles between Swift's fingers.

Their tightness felt a bit like someone holding his hand.

"Look, no one understands your resistance to Justus more than me," said Edric. "But here's the thing: you can't ever let running away be your answer."

Swift stroked the Octopus' slick kraken flesh. "If you think by wanting to make up my own mind, I'm running away—you're dead wrong."

Edric retied the nylon cord around Swift's sleeve, making him shriek. "Not only is running a cowardly move, but it never helps. You'll just wind up someplace else you don't want to be."

Swift distracted himself from the pain by guiding the octopus to climb onto the back of his hand. "You don't know anything about what I want."

"Then tell me what you want." Edric bent to see his face. "Or are you afraid to talk to me, like you're afraid to talk to Justus?"

Edric wasn't afraid to talk to Justus. He never had been intimidated by their father the way the rest of them were. It was Edric, in fact, who, at just two years old, had taken to calling their father by his first name. "Justus."

The name stuck, not just because Edric was so "endearing" at that age, as Mum claimed (Swift couldn't come close to imagining that). But because the title was so fitting.

Justus seemed to be more than a father. Sometimes he seemed more than a man, even. He was, hands down, a "Justus."

But the act of naming their father was just one of the ways Edric bucked convention. Edric refused to let anyone tell him who he was or what he wanted.

And Edric certainly ran from nothing. He tended to run toward conflict, toward danger.

"I'm not running," said Swift. "And I'm no coward. You've seen how I've handled the *Strider* all morning. You can see how I'm going after sailing, going after the Star of Atlantis, without caring what you or anyone thinks."

"Yeah, you are." Edric's face took on a pleased expression, as though he were figuring out a puzzle. "You're bending over backwards, making your life way harder, to avoid bearing a responsibility that very well might belong to you."

"I get to choose whether I try for the Practicum," said Swift.

"If you really meant to try for it—would you tell me?"

Swift studied Edric.

A part of him wanted to confide in Edric; to trust him. But could he?

Edric's expression gentled some. "I'm all ears."

Despite how coarse Edric was, it was probably true that he didn't want to see Swift fail. Edric had guided him safely through these waters. Edric was keeping pressure on his bleeding arm. The pain of his care was unbearable, but—Edric was trying to help. He was helping.

"The thing is..." Swift measured Edric for signs of mockery.

He found none.

"Medicine, as fascinating as it is," said Swift, "it's broken. The stories that Caius comes home with are incredible. But so often, I find myself thinking that doctors go at practicing the wrong way. Don't you think medicine often causes more pain than it heals? I want to read medicine, I really do. But could I take that on? Could I make any difference, or would I just wind up being a cog in a broken machine?"

"Of course medicine's broken," said Edric. "It's imperfect, like everything. And certainly, some doctors practice for the wrong reasons."

"If I were to read medicine, I'd want to figure out where it's not working. I'd want do medicine in a way that only would help, to keep people from suffering needlessly. But I don't know whether any of that's possible."

Edric leaned back, his eyes wide on Swift. "I see it. I couldn't quite before. But I think now I'm seeing what Justus can see."

Could Edric really read him so clearly? He seemed so certain about aspects of Swift, of which Swift himself felt barely aware.

"If you go at medicine," said Edric, "I believe you could

figure out its flaws, their solutions. I bet you could be driven wholly by your own heart."

The *Regulus* passed through the reefs at the far boundary of the cove.

On the deck stood Justus, strong and tall, arms folded, watching, with a father's eyes, his two stranded sons, measuring them, it seemed.

Justus never went at anything but with his whole heart.

"I hope that I would," said Swift.

Edric betrayed half a smile. "Promise me something, Little Brother. Promise me that you'll go after that Practicum with the same spunk I saw in you last night, when you snatched the *Strider*."

Taking the *Strider* had been ten times more difficult, ten times more terrifying than Swift had imagined it would be.

He stared up at Edric.

"What if the Practicum clobbers me? What if I can't pass the entrance trials?"

Justus would be disappointed.

Ash would mock him.

He'd have invested all that time, all that work, only to fail.

"I suppose it will clobber you, if you let it," said Edric. "But just think"—he turned his eyes fully onto Swift—"if you conquered it, you'd rocket out of these days of your boyhood like a jet screaming fire."

Swift's vision dazzled as he gazed at Edric. Dauntless Edric, painting a vision of how he believed Swift might soar.

Edric, watching Swift carefully, asked, "When are you going to tell Justus?" He waved at the *Regulus*. "He's going to be beside himself, you realize, to hear that you're done with the Star of Atlantis."

Those words, "done with the Star of Atlantis," seemed to sink Swift back down to Earth.

Despite the confidence in Swift that Edric was lending, as much as he was boasting of his skill at reading his little brother, Edric only understood Swift halfway.

Swift's vision of growing up, though it might include medicine, seemed tethered to exploration; to wide and wondrous landscapes; to seeking the truth about mythical treasure. To the lore of the Star of Atlantis.

"You have to admit, though, it would be amazing," said Swift. "The Star of Atlantis is history, lost. The fact that no one knows what it is makes it all the more exciting. It's a pretty incredible puzzle to solve, and finding it would bring new knowledge. That's no waste."

Edric looked down at him. "Even if you found something extraordinary, the fact that you were scampering after those myths would tell me that you still are running. If you chase what's sure to amount to nothing, you'll be inviting a world of heartache. But, if you were to go after an honest goal—even one threatening to swamp you—and if you were to succeed...well, that's something."

Swift cupped the baby octopus in his palm. Though she was incredible, she brought a pang of disappointment. For a flash, Swift could see her the way Edric must see her.

She was no mythic sea creature. She was no pirate treasure. Finding her was no legitimate conquest.

Swift lowered the baby to the clear surface of the tide pool and let her plop in.

He studied the divots in the distant round islet.

Unreachable.

The *Regulus* was slipping quickly now through the cove. On its deck, Caius and Trystan were rushing to lower its sails.

Edric guided Swift to standing.

They together watched the *Regulus* close in.

"Justus is wise to have glimpsed this side of you so soon," said Edric. "I will give him that."

Swift steadied himself on Edric's arm. "You didn't listen to Justus. You went your own way."

"That I did. But—though I landed all right..."

Edric's expression shifted to one Swift wasn't used to. He looked as though his defenses were all the way down. Like he was willing to take a punch to the face and not strike back.

"There are things I let go of that I'd give anything to take back." Edric turned his gaze onto Swift. "Justus is right that few lads have the chances you may. I'll sure never reach where you, someday, might."

Swift studied his oldest brother.

He was seeing Edric, really seeing him—and what he saw scared him. He saw sorrow and pain. Disappointment. Regret.

"Don't waste that," said Edric. "Promise me?"

Swift glanced at the cut on his wrist, at Edric's hand tight on it. "I promise."

4

Swift stood closer to Edric as the *Regulus* drew to idling near the islet.

Caius appeared at the big ship's rail holding a coiled rope. He tossed the rope across the gap.

Edric caught it and knotted it to the *Strider's* gunwale.

Swift stumbled into the *Strider* after Edric and sat on her wet bench.

In a moment, the brigantine had the *Strider* towed loose from the eddy's grip. The little dripping ship, pale and gasping, looked like it'd just been resuscitated.

Edric steadied her with the oar while the *Regulus* towed her.

"When are you going to tell Justus you'll go for it?" asked Edric. "If you ask me, there's no sense in putting it off. Might as well be here on all this ocean you love, rather than someplace more common."

The thought of saying the words out loud—*I'll go for the Practicum; I want to read medicine*—felt like trying on shoes too large.

The *Regulus* and the *Strider* together cleared the field of rough waves and reached the border of the cove, where the water evened to shallow rises, the waves only plotting their courses to make landfall.

Caius reeled the *Strider* near enough to the big ship for Edric to snag a ladder of netted rope on its flank.

Edric guided Swift to the net and spotted his climb.

Caius leaned over the rail, his eyes fixed on Swift's hands, his feet, as he placed each inside the knotted squares of rope. "Is that blood on your jacket?"

Swift met Caius' stare. "I scraped my wrist on a screw."

Caius glanced at Edric. "Is he still bleeding?"

"Yeah."

Caius pushed up onto the rail. "Stay where you are, Swift. Don't climb any higher."

"I've got him," said Edric.

"No one has to 'get me,' I can climb by myself." Swift reached for higher ropes and twisted them around his hands. He could pull up just fine, despite the cut. He wedged the toes of his shoes against the next knots.

"I said don't climb." Caius swung over the rail and searched the net with his feet until they found holds.

"You don't have to come down." Swift was a good climber. The best climber among all four brothers. Even if he was a bit dizzy.

Swift pulled himself up to the next knots. "There were tide pools on that islet. In one, we found an octopus that looked like a kraken—"

His shoe slipped. He dropped.

Before he could blink, he found himself swinging free, above Edric's reach, Caius gripping his bloodstained hand.

Caius pulled him back onto the net. He gripped the scruff of Swift's jacket, and in a second, he was over the rail and hauling Swift by the waistline of his trousers across it, to their father.

Caius and Justus knelt before Swift. Caius eased up Swift's sleeve. Blotted the blood off his wrist.

He studied the cut, holding his thumbs firm on either side. Though his grip was tight, though he was even pulling at the cut a little, Swift let him. Caius' fingers, even dealing in pain, were gentle.

Caius glanced up at Swift. "Is this the only place you feel pain?"

"I think so. Will you get to give me stitches?"

"No, but a tetanus shot is probably in order." Caius led him to the bench circling the deck.

"Do we need to head for a clinic?" asked Trystan.

"It's not too bad," said Caius. "It just needs to be cleaned and buttoned up."

A droplet of blood cascaded down and pooled hot in Swift's palm. He wobbled as the *Regulus* swayed.

Trystan steadied him. "He's going white as the sails." He glanced at Justus. "You sure medicine is where you want this one?"

"He's been on the sea since before dawn." Justus, watching Swift carefully, pulled a first aid bag from under the bench. "Of course he'd be spent."

Caius drew out an antiseptic wipe and tore it open.

Swift's stomach dropped at Caius spreading apart his split skin.

He doubled at the sting of Caius cleaning it.

Edric took hold of Swift around the chest and held him while Caius blotted the length of the cut, even the red inside, with stinking brown fluid.

Swift clung to Edric until the shadow of the pain faded from his sight.

"Heads up," said Edric. "Lad's going green."

Caius glanced up at Swift. "You gonna chunder?"

Swallowing down nausea, Swift shook his head.

Caius dried the cut and fastened it with a series of butterfly bandages.

With the cut tended and concealed, Swift's nausea dimmed.

He found his gaze drawn to the middle of the deck, where a catastrophe of laminated maps, pinned by rocks, littered the planks.

These were maps he'd laid out from his father's stow,

showing the water courses along the Welsh coast, illustrating currents and weather and winds.

One of them was the article from the school gazette—the interview of Ash.

Near Swift's feet, firm under a stone, fluttered a hand-drawn map. A map from his one remaining pirate treasure book, *The Star of Atlantis*.

It displayed the shape of a cove where apparently the lost treasure rested—Sterncastle Cove.

Even though the map had no coordinates or specific directions, it was drawn in close detail, every rock, every nook on the coastline intricate.

Swift eased the map out from under its stone.

Along its edge lay the oath of the Star of Atlantis, scribed in curling letters that looked born of waves. And beneath those words, cryptic markings were drawn. Markings that looked like the letters of some language, lost.

And here, too, was the only guidance Swift had—wonderful, though obscure—about where the Star of Atlantis lay hidden.

When the shore draws long and straight, skim the briny banks. Be swallowed by Sterncastle Cove. Seek the islet, round as Earth, studded with Kraken fangs. Mind the deeps for mermaid tails, shimmering blue and green. Heed their song, but touch the water not, lest your life be forfeit to their goddess. Always keep a weather eye on the mist coiling in the cove, for through it paddles old Grog Blossom, always dead, yet ever awake, cursed to forever sail as watchman over the Star of Atlantis.

Swift fixed on the mesmerizing words, their images, as Caius snipped a round of gauze and slid it over Swift's hand, snugging it around the cut.

The immediacy of the map—this expanse of sea rocking the *Regulus*, this gilded line of Welsh coast—his father and brothers still on the ship with him, still clad in gear for sailing, for treasure hunting—it all brought his longing for the Star of Atlantis rushing back.

His talk with Edric, all that honesty he'd manipulated out of Swift, seemed abstract again. Grossly misfitting here.

Swift glanced at his father, whose shared love for the sea was the very fuel that'd stirred them all up today for treasure chasing.

Justus, though, wasn't looking at Swift anymore, nor at the wild waters, nor at the stretch of northerly coves. He was fiddling with his phone.

If he could get Justus speaking about the treasure, maybe he'd grow interested again.

"Where'd you first hear of the Star of Atlantis?" asked Swift.

"From a fisherman who used to work the stretch of the water near Grandfather's house." Justus, tapping his phone, leaned against the mast. "He was a strange fellow—a hermit. I liked to fish with him off the dock there. Then came the day when someone reported that the Star of Atlantis had been found. A chest full of silver, it was said to be."

"That had to be codswallop," said Swift. "Did anyone believe it?"

"It was a phony rumor to be sure." Justus chuckled. "Following that, we did our share of combing beaches for the Star of Atlantis, dreaming of finding the real thing."

Even though he was speaking of the Star of Atlantis, Justus' eyes were no longer pale and washed with wonder, as they'd been since dawn. They were bespectacled and hard focused on his phone.

Caius and Trystan, too, had stopped looking north to the coves, to the wonderful, tide-washed coves.

Instead, they were readying the sails to swell and pull them landward.

Swift's heart, though, still thundered at the mere notion of chasing that northern horizon, to see if just perhaps they could find a shore drawing long and straight; to see if they might discover Sterncastle Cove, studded with its kraken fangs and cherishing an islet, round as Earth, promising the Star of Atlantis.

The only other creatures on the ship, though, who seemed

to share his draw to venturing on were two ravens perched on the rail.

Fluttering up and back down again as the wind twisted, they seemed never to remove their keen black eyes from the line of coves further north, with ribbons of white water shining.

Perhaps these ravens had been part of the flock that'd circled the dead maybe-Kraken. In their travels, they might've even flown over the Star of Atlantis.

Caius returned and snugged Swift's sleeve over the bandage. "You warm enough?"

Swift traced the oath on his map. "Seems the weather might hold out for us to have a go at one more cove."

"We've gone about as far as we can on sheer luck, wouldn't you say?" asked Caius, his eyes tired and a bit cold with the honesty.

At a wind rising, the ravens together stumbled off the rail.

Swift watched them fly up and off.

Caius wasn't wrong. Even using Swift's book, this map, they had little to go on to figure out Sterncastle Cove's true location. A good deal of research would be needed to brighten his prospects.

But to stop now, to abandon these wilds, to forsake their mysteries—it felt like smothering a piece of himself just as true as the part that loved medicine.

Swift captured his father's glance. "What would you say to trying one more?"

Though Justus did look at him, his eyes weren't really seeing Swift anymore. They were distanced, the way they went whenever he started thinking about work.

An anesthesiologist—known to be one of the best in the country—Justus spent a great deal of time researching his patients' cases. Maybe too much time.

Justus, messing with his phone, eased past Swift, to Caius. "I'd like a look at the hospital roster, to see what I'm in for tomorrow. But I can't manage to pick up a signal."

"No chance of a signal this far out, probably." Caius took the phone and toyed with it.

"I have a good feeling about that cove, just at the horizon." Swift waited for Justus to look at him.

"Lad." Edric wound in the anchor. "What did we just talk about?"

Holding his map, Swift felt like he still had a grip on the wilder part of himself. A part he wanted to keep.

"I haven't been out searching with father," said Swift.

Trystan glanced north. "There's a smell of rain on the wind. I say we'd better get home."

"This feels nothing like storm wind." Swift hurried to the middle of the deck, where the maps and guides lay.

Edric followed him.

Sea venturing was right at Swift's fingertips. And here on the *Regulus*, in the company of his father, of magnificent Caius, who'd been able to make sense of the cut—the course to medicine was seeming more and more out of reach.

"Swift?" Edric lifted his brow. "Isn't it time to change course?"

Caius, staring at Edric, gave Justus back his phone. "What's going on?"

Swift looked up at his father, at each of his brothers.

A weekend of sailing with them, at his request, had been extraordinary. He'd been flying, all night and all morning, his quick heart beating with the sails.

But now, the way Edric was looking at him—the way they all were looking at him—the magic seemed almost worn off.

Swift knelt among the maps. "We still have a little time for exploring." He cast his gaze to the enchantment of never-ending waters, of sea birds crying, of distant coves, untried, hiding treasure foretold by legends.

Watching it all, it seemed tides within him were rising, allying his heart with the sea.

Edric knelt in front of him. "I thought you'd managed to get a grip on yourself."

And this sort of venture might never happen again. Today might be the very last day of his boyhood.

"There's definitely time to try another cove," said Swift.

"By what you told me on that islet," said Edric, low, "I saw for myself that medicine is true to who you are."

That part of Swift that Edric had seen was seeming slippery here. The treasure-hunting part of himself, Swift was sure of.

"Medicine was true to who I am," said Swift. "It is true. It's just—"

"Then tell him," said Edric.

Justus advanced. "I'd like to know what all this is about."

Caius did the father's work of glaring Swift to standing.

"It's just that Edric and I spoke a little," said Swift.

Trystan approached. "And?"

"And I told him..." The map felt suddenly slick in Swift's hands, sweat wetting it. "I want to do medicine." Swift held the map closer to his chest against an uptick of wind. "I want to do the Practicum, but—"

"Well, that's wonderful!" said Justus.

Caius glanced at Edric. "He told you this—honestly?"

"I thought you might delay." Justus' smile seemed as wide as the horizon.

"He did tell me honestly." Edric, looking down at Swift, seemed pleased. "You two have him pegged right."

Swift took a deep breath. "The Practicum is what I want. But can I not want more than one thing?"

A bluster of hard wind swept the deck.

The gale wrangled up one of the maps, poorly held by its stone, and sent it flying.

It was a map charting patterns of currents on the Celtic Sea.

Trystan and Justus rushed to try to catch it.

The map caught on the *Regulus'* rail.

It held still for a second, but another burst of wind sent it soaring.

Swift watched its form flap—a geometric print of blue and white against a bright summer sky growing clouded.

It lifted, fluttering crookedly like the broken wing of a bird.

Swift gazed over the wide sea upheaving unplundered islets and coves. He gazed at the summer sky, its daylight shrouding stars.

He admired the rollicking wind and waves, somewhere whispering near to the Star of Atlantis.

The map drifted down to the north and coasted toward a whole string of coves they'd not tried, their bases turquoise with eddies.

Swift watched the map's play on the waves—flattening to mercurial deepness when they troughed, then shining nickel-silver when they crested.

Watching his father's map sail off, beyond reach—something inside Swift seemed to break. He held closer his own map, to the Star of Atlantis.

Caius dislodged the map from Swift's hands and folded it.

"Why don't you help me steer?" asked Trystan.

Justus climbed to the steering deck with Trystan and held out his arm. "Lad. Come."

Swift went to him.

"Look lively, Swift," said Trystan, his face soft with the gentle smile that never really left him. "We'll come back to the sea again." He trained Swift's hands on the wheel.

The map of sea currents was now floating a good distance from the ship.

Swift stared at it, flat and white, mounting wave after wave.

He put all his effort into envisioning severing his spirit and leaving it behind with that map, fluttering on the blue water— pinned there like the lobbed-off shadow of Peter Pan.

The *Regulus* moved out of a haze of spray, and the Welsh coast clarified in strong detail.

That brown dock approaching, the commonplace encroaching, felt worse than the night the summer holidays ended.

With every nautical mile they crossed, Swift's sense of alliance with the sea slipped until the glimmer of waiting treasure seemed something he'd only imagined.

Leaning against Trystan, steady behind him, Swift felt just a shell.

It was as though his spirit really had been cast into the Celtic Sea, to linger there, abandoned, beside a treasure he never would chase.

5

Swift, sitting at the kitchen table, couldn't unglue his eyes from the TV, showing the local news.

His hands—one clenched around a bottle of anti-nausea meds, the other tangled in a stethoscope, tightened into fists.

He'd been tasked to do Caius the favor of organizing his medical bag. He was to take out what was expired and place new date labels on the fresh supplies.

Caius stepped in. "Looks like you've made some progress."

"No way," Swift whispered. "There's no way."

Staring at Swift, Caius went to the fridge. "Is something wrong?"

Swift didn't respond.

Caius lifted out a beer bottle. "Hey, you all right?"

"It's just—" Swift pointed at the screen. "This isn't possible."

There, on a Welsh beach, speaking into microphones held by a dozen reporters—stood Ash. Beside him stood Mr. Emberly, his father.

"What the blazes?" Caius sat.

Swift turned up the volume.

"Inside this cave, right behind us"—Ash glanced over his shoulder—"that's where I found it."

The reporters shouted questions.

Ash looked down, as though shy. As though overwhelmed by the fuss.

Though a genuine-seeming bashfulness claimed the better part of his expression, it failed to conceal a bright mirth in his eyes. Ash was loving this.

The question which Ash seemed to catch was, "What was inside the treasure chest you found?"

Swift threw down the meds. "Son of a cock up."

"Hey," said Caius. "Mouth."

"The chest is under analysis," said Ash. "The museum curator I spoke with thinks it dates back to the great days of Welsh piracy. I found it intact, buried beneath stones, and locked. I can only speculate about what might be in it, but I'm pretty sure it's valuable. It's thought to be from the same era as other key treasures, known still to be lost."

It'd been just a few weeks since Swift had gone fruitlessly chasing after the Star of Atlantis.

He'd worked hard not to think about his seafaring ambitions, instead spending his time helping Caius and reading through a couple of anatomy books, plus a few texts on biochemistry Justus had given him.

And all that while, Ash had been treasure hunting. Treasure finding.

"What are you hoping the chest holds?" asked a reporter.

A dapper grin spread across Ash's face. "Gold. Silver. Coins. Jewels. Leads to more treasures."

In the corner of the screen, there appeared a picture of a time-worn box—the treasure chest Ash had found.

It was cobbled of dark wood and about the size of a toaster oven. It was sealed by a series of metal clamps.

Swift clenched the stethoscope. "That's exactly what I imagined pirate treasure would look like."

"If it does contain anything of value, what will you do with it?" asked a reporter.

Ash studied his feet a moment, then swept his gaze across his audience.

He looked like a professional actor, or a model. He looked like he'd practiced this.

"To be honest, as cool as it was, finding that chest"—Ash paused—"this wasn't the treasure I was after."

"What were you after?" they all asked at once.

"Something much more valuable." Ash held his gaze low a moment, then looked straight into the camera.

It felt as though he were looking right at Swift. As though he knew Swift was watching.

"I've spent years reading about the age of Norse pirates and the rarest treasures their legends describe." Ash drew out an old book—one of the old books he'd stolen from Swift.

"Bloody Helheim." Swift stood, sending bottles of medicine rolling.

Ash smiled. "I aim to go after the Star of Atlantis."

Swift smacked the table. "No!"

Edric wandered in. "What's going on?"

Swift threaded his fingers into his hair. "How could he do this to me?"

Edric sat on the edge of the table. "What the...is that Ash?"

"Swift's old buddy had some luck treasure hunting," said Caius. "Says he's going after the Star of Atlantis."

Edric shook his head. "Son of a cock up."

"I've never been great in school." Ash, his dark hair blowing back from his forehead, caught his father's eye. "I have a different sort of mind, I've been told."

"A different sort of mind," mumbled Swift. "He just won't do the work. I've watched him slack off for five years."

"I think I've found what I truly am good at," said Ash. "Solving mysteries of the past—I think that's my thing. And though the contents of the chest aren't fully understood, I feel really good about one thing—it seems they might serve as clues to help me onto my next find."

"What sort of clues?" asked a reporter.

Ash's smile was smug. "I'm not at liberty to talk about that. What I want to say, though, is this. It feels good to know, now, that I can just be myself."

Ash looked again straight at the camera. "I don't have to claim I'll be a doctor for my father to be proud of me."

Mr. Emberly pulled Ash into a hug.

The crowd of reporters shouted questions, but Ash only waved as Mr. Emberly drew him away.

The camera stayed on him as he walked beside his father, along a sunsetted strip of Welsh beach.

Words appeared at the bottom of the screen: "Brilliant boy finds lost pirate treasure."

Caius set his hand on Swift's shoulder.

Swift just stood stiff, unable to remove his gaze from the brilliant boy using books that he'd stolen to chase after a dream Swift had sparked.

A dream Swift was trying to let go of.

Swift stared at his brothers. "How could he?"

"Don't take it as personal." Edric slid into a chair beside Caius. "It's not like you own sole rights to go after the Star of Atlantis."

"That was my bloody book."

"Well, that is pretty shitty," said Edric.

"I remember that book," said Swift. "I read it several times. It's on Welsh history—it says nothing about the Star of Atlantis. Ash had to have brought it out only for show."

"Really, though, what else would you expect from Ash?" Caius gently unwound the stethoscope from among Swift's fingers. "He's always been cruel to you."

"I doubt he was even thinking about you," said Edric.

"Did you not hear what he said?" asked Swift. "That he doesn't have to become a doctor for his father to be proud of him. Justus and Mum are keeping an eye on their house since they've been in Wales. Justus spoke with Mr. Emberly yesterday. I heard him talking about my plan to try and test into the Practicum."

"If Ash was taking a swing at you," said Edric, "your job is to not let the strike land."

"He was definitely taking a swing at me."

"The bottom line is that you do have a plan," said Caius. "A good one. Edric's right—you can forget Ash."

"I'll forget him." Swift narrowed his eyes at the screen, still showing pictures of the treasure chest, of the brilliant boy. "I'll do my research. I'll beat him to the Star of Atlantis."

Caius and Edric exchanged glances.

"But wouldn't it lead to nothing?" Edric leaned in. "Let Ash do all the stupid goose chasing. You have a better course, right?"

"I'll leave him in the dust." Swift couldn't blink.

"If he was thinking of you when he said that doctor bit"—Edric snapped to capture Swift's gaze—"then that lad's manipulating you into competing with him. I'm telling you—don't take that bait."

"This isn't about competition," said Swift. "It's about standing up for myself."

"I see the fire of competition all over your face," said Eric. "If you bite, Ash wins."

"Edric is right," said Caius. "You've moved on to a serious, amazing endeavor. Ash is still in a place of petty pursuits."

Petty pursuits.

"I thought you wanted to see me stand my ground," said Swift.

Edric shrugged. "Not if it means letting that lad get the better of you."

Swift threw up his arms. "Then what was all that talk, when we were marooned on the islet, about how you want me to stop running away?"

"Letting this go—that isn't running," said Edric. "It's being the bigger person."

Swift shifted his gaze onto Caius. "Will you help me?"

"Even if I took you sailing, even if you researched leads"—Caius glanced at Edric—"the Star of Atlantis—it just isn't out there. I'm afraid that it's bound to be lost."

Swift held on to his stomach.

The void of having let go of the Star of Atlantis felt vacuous. And with Caius and Edric refusing him any support, he felt he might collapse inward like a star that can no longer bear its own burn.

"Finding the Star of Atlantis might be difficult," said Swift. "But it's not impossible, right?"

Caius said nothing. He only held himself very thoughtfully.

But there was a sparkle in Caius' eye.

Of course there was.

And of course there was a small smile at the corner of his mouth.

Caius was smart enough to know what a trap it is to declare something wholly impossible.

At the trauma hospital, he managed the impossible every day.

He knew how to maintain a glimmer of hopefulness, no matter what.

If Edric had been teaching Swift not to run, Caius had been teaching him not to despair.

"I know that you haven't resigned the Star of Atlantis as lost," said Swift, to Caius. "I can see it in your eyes. You'd like to go after it with me."

"Even if you found something," said Edric, "what would an old pirate relic do for you?" He clicked off the TV. "The real opportunity here is to learn to keep Ash from getting to you."

Even though Edric was missing the point, he wasn't wrong. Ash always had targeted Swift.

He needed to get free of that.

Swift drifted down into his chair. "A few weeks after the Tumble—that night when Ash cornered me in the oak woods— he said something I can't forget. He said that as he fell into the water, he read on my face that I wanted him dead. He told me he thinks that I'm jealous of him." He turned his eyes onto Caius. "He's using that old grudge to take swing after swing."

"He's a mean kid," said Caius. "I thought so long before the Tumble. You'll recall that the books weren't the first thing he stole from you. Anytime he'd spend the night, he'd make off with something or other from your room."

"That lad's troubled," said Edric. "He's been troubled since his mum left. She abandoned him and Mr. Emberly not a week before the Tumble. It's no surprise he's gone haywire, with everything he's been through—getting a bit mean, a bit jealous."

"That's all the more reason that I can't let him get away with this," said Swift. "If Ash aims to go after the Star of Atlantis, then so must I."

"Ten minutes ago, the Star of Atlantis was out of your mind," said Edric. "And now, suddenly, you're telling us you have to go after it?"

"Ash is stealing my dream," said Swift. "I'm not going to let him."

Edric glanced at Caius' med bag, at Swift's handwriting on the medicine labels. "I thought your dream was to follow Justus. To follow Caius."

Swift picked up the stethoscope. He righted a few scattered bottles. "Can I not have two dreams?"

"Look, you're about to dive very deeply into studying," said Caius. "For a long while, you'll have no time for anything but prepping for your exams and entrance trials."

"It'll be weeks before I can really begin," said Swift. "I can't even get the materials until I turn fourteen. Justus said we'd start in after his holiday with Mum. I could use that time to research the Star of Atlantis."

"But it just isn't out there," said Edric. "I say, try to accept that. When you admit to yourself that it's truly a lost cause, Ash's manipulations won't be able to touch you."

Caius and Edric were both sounding sensible, and some of the points they were making were solid.

But the fact was—the Star of Atlantis was widely believed to be more than a myth. And it had never been found.

Seeing, by Ash's discovery, what finding a treasure actually looked like...seeing that it was possible...

"The thing is," said Swift, "it just might be out there."

If he didn't try, and if Ash found the Star of Atlantis...

"I'm doing this," said Swift, "whether you two like it or not. And if you'd help me go out on the water, I'd have a better chance."

Caius set to work, loading his supplies back into his med bag.

"Well, I'm out." Edric stood. "Opening a second brewery—it's four times as much work as keeping just the one going."

Swift eased the med bag away from Caius. "Doesn't a part of you, at least, want to do this?"

"I'm not even sure Mum and Justus would let me take you sailing alone," said Caius.

"Come on, Mum and Justus trust you."

"It would be very difficult, sailing the *Regulus* with just two," said Edric. "You'd be in for a lot of exhaustion and a good measure of disappointment."

Swift rested the stethoscope inside the med bag. "If I don't do this, I'll regret it. Forever."

Caius studied him a moment. "I'd need you to assure me that you understand Edric's point. Your research, as strong as it's bound to be, won't likely yield much. You'd need to accept that from the outset."

"Is that a *yes*?"

Swift stood.

Caius lifted from the corner of the table Swift's *Star of Atlantis* book. "I'll tell you what. You do your research. Find any leads that you can. Since you won't start in on concertedly studying for a few weeks—"

"I don't like where this is going," said Edric.

"—and if Mum and Justus are okay with it," said Caius, "we'll take a weekend of sailing to celebrate your birthday. Sort of a last hurrah before you start prepping."

Swift's heart skipped into a run.

"Justus is hitting his busiest season at work," said Edric, to Caius. "You realize he couldn't go with you?"

"I don't think he'd need to," said Caius. "Swift and I make a good team."

"Well it's going to be a trick getting Mum to buy in," said Edric.

Caius shrugged. "Really, why wouldn't she? They'll be traveling all over the South of France the weekend of his birthday.

It'd be Swift and me making trouble around here, if not in Wales."

Swift could hardly contain his smile. Caius wasn't agreeing to do this just to placate him.

Caius was wanting to do this.

Caius believed they had a shot.

"Mum and Justus might even see it as good for Swift to have something to look forward to," said Caius, "considering the degree of hard work ahead of him."

"I think the both of you are taking this too far," said Edric. "Bottom line—it's a fool's chase."

"If your research turns up nothing, we'll just sail and camp." Caius nudged Swift. "That'd be okay, right?"

A weekend for just the two of them, sailing together. Camping beneath the stars on the Welsh coast. Seeking the Star of Atlantis together.

Putting Ash in his place.

"My research is going to come through for us," said Swift.

"I don't like the thought of you two out on the North Atlantic on your own," said Edric. "I doubt Justus will like the idea any better. And Mum certainly won't."

"But if you help, they're sure to say yes," said Swift. "Justus always listens to you."

Edric rolled his eyes. "If I do decide to help, I'll argue that this absurd chase might be the only way to get treasure hunting out of your system. For good."

"So that's it?" Swift glanced from Edric to Caius. "We're really doing this?"

"On one condition," said Caius.

Swift tossed up his Star of Atlantis book and caught it. "Anything!"

"I'd like you to go to Ash and congratulate him."

Swift dropped his book. "Anything but that."

"You need to let him know," said Caius, "in no uncertain terms, that he isn't getting to you."

Swift slipped into his seat. "No way."

"Caius is dead right," said Edric. "Flattering that narcissist is the best way—probably the only way—to get him to leave you alone."

"And exactly what am I supposed to congratulate him on?" asked Swift. "Stealing my books? Snatching my dream? Finding a way to provoke and insult me on the news?"

"Tell him that you think his find is amazing," said Caius. "Let him talk to you about it."

"Whatever you do, though," said Edric, "don't let on that you have any intention to go after the Star of Atlantis."

Swift picked up his book. "That's about the only thing I do want to tell him."

"If you let that slip," said Edric, "he'll think you're playing right into his hands."

Swift slid his book onto the table. "Why can't I just leave him be? What's wrong with staying out of his way?"

"You mean running?" asked Edric.

Swift opened the book and drew out its map.

"If you congratulate Ash on his find," said Caius, "if you let him see plainly that you've moved on, he'll realize you're no longer threatened by him. It'll take all the fun out of his game."

"One more thing," said Edric. "Are you certain he knows you'll be trying for the Practicum?"

"He definitely knows," said Swift. "Justus said Ash was with Mr. Emberly when they were talking about it."

"Congratulate the little tosser, as soon as he's back from Wales," said Edric. "Ask him about his discovery. Let him have his moment." He leaned in. "If he returns the favor and cares to be interested in your plans—if he congratulates you, which he should—that'll be a sign he's getting past this idiotic rivalry."

"And if he doesn't bring up the Practicum?" asked Swift.

"You'll have been the bigger person," said Caius. "You'll have done all you can. Enough, perhaps, that he'll leave you alone from here on out."

Being the bigger person might be somewhat rewarding.

But maybe, by congratulating Ash, there'd be an even better payoff.

Maybe Ash would boast about what was in the chest he

found. Maybe he'd betray what he'd learned about the Star of Atlantis.

Edric drew the map to *The Star of Atlantis* away from Swift and glanced it over. Caius seemed unable to take his eyes off the cover of the book, with its brilliant seven-pointed Celtic star.

Swift found he couldn't take his eyes off of Caius and Edric —his brothers, helping him toward a dream that was as much a part of him as medicine.

Swift ran his fingers along the worn corners of his book.

This contained clues to the Star of Atlantis that Ash knew nothing about. And Swift was light years beyond Ash in understanding how to research. He could handily drum up more leads.

He'd have to talk to Ash, yes. But he had what he needed to conquer him.

After Swift beat Ash to the Star of Atlantis, there'd be no more dodging anyone. And no longer would he have to tolerate accusations from Edric that he was running.

When Swift sailed back to Clovelly, successful and bearing his treasure, there might be a team of reporters crowded on the dock, waiting.

The whole world would see how important the Star of Atlantis was. And how profound was the achievement of finding it.

Maybe even Edric would see it. Maybe Justus would.

6

Swift hurried out of his house in the gleam of daybreak.

This bright Thursday dawn marked three weeks to the day since he'd promised Caius and Edric that he'd talk to Ash, that he'd be the bigger person and try to get free of him.

Ash was finally back in Clovelly, and the last three weeks, waiting for this moment, had been agony—Swift dreading its nearing; imagining what Ash might say; looking forward to the closure this might bring.

Trekking down Clovelly's main road—cobbled with round stones and winding down to the sea, Swift glanced back toward his house.

Everyone in his family was still asleep, except Edric, who'd left before daylight to take care of some chores for his brewery.

Mum, slipping out of her room for a moment, while it was still dark, had caught Swift preparing to leave for the marina, where Ash was likely to be.

She'd told him that he looked tired, and that he should take it easy instead of fooling around by the docks at dawn.

But being tired had never precluded him from going at an ambition. And Swift couldn't imagine taking anything easy. Not with so much in front of him.

This was the very weekend Caius was taking him sailing. Thinking of it, Swift had hardly been able to sleep.

And sleep was yet harder to reach, knowing that today was the day he'd face Ash.

Today was the day for being the bigger person. For showing Ash that his manipulations weren't working.

And maybe for catching some leads Ash might drop.

Caius and Edric thought Swift had no hope of getting anywhere on that score and shouldn't even try. "Don't sink to his level," Caius had said. And Edric: "If you can read him like that, don't you think the little twerp can read you just as well? Keep it civil."

And Ash could read Swift.

It was both the best and the worst thing about people who've known each other since childhood—Swift and Ash knew one another so instinctively, it was nearly impossible to hide anything.

But Swift might indeed be clever enough to get something from Ash without showing his own cards.

If Ash let slip anything he knew, any research he'd done, if Swift could get him prattling about what was in that treasure chest—any small risk of vulnerability would be worth it.

Swift hurried through the bustle of the downtown Clovelly shops, just opening.

He slowed as he passed a display of old books, eyeing it for anything he hadn't seen before—anything on sailing or sea lore.

Though Swift hadn't reached any certain conclusions about the whereabouts of Sterncastle Cove, he'd uncovered a few insights and was well on track with his research.

He'd learned more of the history of the Star of Atlantis— why it was stolen and how it was prized. And he'd gotten ahold of an old woodblock print of what was thought to be a picture of what Sterncastle Cove actually looked like.

That woodblock print seemed critically important and a very lucky, rare find.

It'd come from a hand-made Welsh sailing guide, used by members of some clan—people claiming to keep knowledge of where historical Welsh treasures, including the Star of Atlantis, were stowed.

Swift cleared the whitewashed shops, with their calligraphied signs, with their flowers and greens spilling from pots jeweling windows and doorways, and moved into the northern openness that stretched from Devonshire's coast to the broad waterline of the blue Bristol Channel.

From here, the rolling sea shone, providing a sapphire backdrop for the ships gently cruising. Low storm clouds, gray and blushing apricot, brought out the sky's petrels and gulls in relief.

Watching the water sway made Swift dizzy, almost delirious, with a swelling desire to ride it with Caius.

Swift pulled his gaze off the water and glanced around the beach. Ash's father docked their motorboat in this marina, and here, Ash often could be found.

And there, sure enough, sat Ash. He'd pulled the tarp off his father's motorboat and was resting on its bench.

The media had released a small article each week about Ash, along with the latest on his discovery. But the articles never revealed what his treasure chest held. The cave where Ash had found it fell under no jurisdiction, and so it was essentially his. So far, he'd been determined to keep it a secret.

That seemed evidence that it really did have something to do with the Star of Atlantis.

Swift hurried on, over a flat stretch of sand, making for a broad lifeguarding platform.

Around its edge, he studied his former best friend.

Ash seemed to be reading something. Was he researching?

No. The book Ash was thumbing through was a comic. He looked relaxed, like he was simply soaking up what sun would be out today.

The sea was indeed pressing a wind that would soon blow those blue clouds to storm.

Good. If Ash felt at liberty to take it easy, Swift—hard focused on research and planning—would have an edge in the chase to the Star of Atlantis.

Swift came out from behind the lifeguarding platform. He

took his time walking down the beach to the dock, like he was perfectly at ease.

He stopped before Ash's boat.

Ash looked up. "Whoa." He stripped off his sunglasses. "Swift. You're the last person I thought I'd see today."

"I heard you'd come back from Wales," said Swift.

Ash climbed out of the boat. "This morning, before the sun was even up, several cars passed my house, driving slowly—as though they were spying through our windows. I had to get out of there. I needed to be someplace where I could have some anonymity."

Swift worked to refrain from rolling his eyes. They weren't even one minute into their meeting, and Ash had already set this up as a drama—he the pressured celebrity, Swift the nuisance.

Ash scanned the shore as though watching for the paparazzi. "I'm doing my best to avoid crowded places. Probably, you won't be the only person trying to find me today."

Swift glanced around the marina. It was always bustling this early, with sailors tending their boats and preparing to set out.

There were plenty of people here—but not one of them was looking at Ash.

"Reporters have been calling my father incessantly," said Ash, "asking, 'When is Ash venturing out next? What was in his treasure chest?' The question no reporter can stay away from is: 'Does he have any insights on what the Star of Atlantis might be?' It's like they think that just because I've found one priceless treasure, I'm capable of making guesses about others."

Swift bit his lip, holding back an impulse to rattle off that it didn't matter what Ash thought the Star of Atlantis might be because he was never going to lay his hands on it.

Ash tossed the comic book into the boat. "But now here you are. You, of course, would know where to find me."

"I can leave, if you want," said Swift.

Which he wouldn't. Of all people, Swift was probably the one Ash would like to crow over the most.

Ash shrugged. "I guess this is the sort of thing I'll have to get used to—people seeking me out now that I have some legitimate fame."

Swift waited a moment, to gauge whether that could possibly be a joke, Ash comically exaggerating.

A span of silence pronounced that Ash was serious.

"Your legitimate fame isn't why I came," said Swift.

"Why did you come?"

Swift studied Ash a moment. What would be the best approach to get him talking explicitly about his find?

"I just wanted to say"—Swift lifted Ash's hand and shook it—"congratulations."

Ash, smirking, took back his hand. "This must be killing you."

Swift settled his hands in his pockets; took an easy stance. "Not at all. The truth is, I'm happy for you. I've pretty much put treasure hunting behind me."

Ash crinkled his brow. "I don't buy that."

"I mean, I do read about treasure chases and legends, sometimes," said Swift. "It's not that I'm no longer interested. In fact, I've been curious about the treasure chest you found."

"You're curious—because you're just casually interested?"

"Is there something wrong with that?" asked Swift.

"If you're only 'casually interested,' I feel that's my fault." Ash leaned on a dock post. "I've been told that when I found my historic piece in Wales, some long-time treasure hounds simply gave up their hunts. I guess they felt a sense of overwhelming discouragement. Most treasures, you see, are found by people who've already made a discovery. People who have, as I call it, 'the knack.' And I did collect one of what might only be three or four maritime treasures that are actually out there."

Swift had to lower his gaze to his shoes to keep a smile off his face.

Ash clearly had done little research if he thought "historic pieces" were scarce. They were difficult to find, yes. But the truth was that every generation, going back thousands upon thousands of years, had left plenty of rubbish lying around.

Ash had no idea what he was dealing in.

"So, about that treasure chest." Swift glanced up at Ash. "Have you told anyone what was in it?"

"No. But, oh, man, I wish I could tell you, of all people. You—someone so interested in the Star of Atlantis."

Swift examined Ash's expression for any hints that, with enough needling, he'd spill.

But nothing suggested that he wanted Swift to pry.

Was that because the treasure Ash found was terribly valuable? Or could there be just junk inside, or nothing at all? Or maybe the museum had determined that it wasn't actually connected in any significant way with Norse pirate lore.

But Ash did seem to be enjoying keeping his secret. This clandestine show might actually mean that Ash's find was really excellent. That it was linked to the Star of Atlantis.

"You mention the Star of Atlantis," said Swift. "Surely whatever you found can't really be part of that myth. I mean—if we don't know what the Star of Atlantis is, how could anyone speculate that what you found is related?"

Ash narrowed his eyes. "If you've given up the hunt, why do you care so much?"

Encounters with Ash always brought on an uncomfortable heat. And, sure enough, now Swift was sweating.

Concentrating on keeping his body from overheating was usually helpful in maintaining a grip on himself.

Swift drew his hands out of his pockets. "It's precisely because I've given up the hunt that I care. It's like asking someone to show you how a puzzle is worked once you've given up on trying to solve it."

Ash smirked. "You've never in your life given up on a puzzle."

There was a sickening pleasure on Ash's face. It was like he was enjoying withholding what he knew Swift wanted.

And of course, Ash hadn't brought up Swift's Practicum plans. And he certainly wouldn't.

"As it turns out," said Swift, "I, too, might have a 'knack.' But for something bigger than anything I've tried before."

"You can give up that coy act." Ash let slip a grin. "I know what you're up to."

Was he talking about Swift's plan to go after the Star of Atlantis with Caius?

Surely not. Right?

Swift half-stepped back. "What do you mean?"

"Your father talked to mine."

But Justus wouldn't have betrayed Swift. Right?

"About?"

"About that Practicum thingy you're doing," said Ash.

Swift let go of a held breath.

Ash seemed to be reading him, noting the relief.

Unlike Swift, Ash always seemed ordered and ice cool. And he was handling this encounter—which had to be uncomfortable for him, too—with poise.

That trick of staying chilled under pressure was one of the reasons Ash was so popular at school. He knew that Swift dealt with anxiety, and this was one of the many differences he misused to prove to Swift that he could outdo him.

"Does your father know you've given up on the Star of Atlantis?" asked Ash." It seems that might disappoint him."

Swift rubbed the back of his neck. "What would you know about my father?"

"When he called us, he talked way more about me and my treasure than you and your Practicum plans. And he said that my own father should be very proud. That he'd be so proud of me if I were his son."

Swift pushed up his sleeves.

"I imagine it's tough on a parent," said Ash, "watching their kid go after something they'll probably fail at."

Failing the entrance exams for the Practicum was a real possibility. And even if Swift passed them, he'd have to remain in top form to keep his place, to secure university scholarships.

If Swift were the finder of the Star of Atlantis, then at least he'd have that to fall back on, if he did fail the exams—if he failed at medicine altogether.

Ash wasn't wrong that finding the treasure might make

Justus, and everyone, view him as important and special in other ways.

"Justus doesn't believe that I'm going to fail," said Swift.

"Well, he wouldn't say as much to you, right?" asked Ash. "He's your father. But he did tell my father straight up that it's highly improbable you'll get accepted."

Surely, Justus never would've said anything of the sort.

"The odds are steep, yes." Swift worked to meter his breathing. "But I feel good about trying."

"Oh. If trying is all you want, then you'll be all right."

Swift felt somewhat stunned that Ash was taking his brutality so far. It was clear that his game was to swipe every bit of the wind from Swift's sails, to crack his every ambition.

"Because even if you made it into the Practicum," said Ash, "it seems improbable that you'd do well."

A panic set in.

A panic of being seen, as through a transparent skin. A panic of Ash recognizing Swifts deepest insecurities and exploiting them.

Swift watched the cool, blue clouds coasting in until he felt some of the heat in his chest fade.

"I know I could do well in the Practicum."

Ash tensed, like he was struggling to keep a straight face. "If you say so."

Swift tried to keep his voice calm, his tone friendly, his face cool as he asked—"What's that supposed to mean?"

Ash glanced back at the water, its surface roughening some with a rising wind. "I've seen you seasick. A lot. Seems you might have a weak stomach." He went to the stern of his father's boat and drew out the tarp. "Not that there's anything wrong with having a weak stomach. But—you can't even handle slicing open a mackerel."

Swift widened his collar. "I don't think the Practicum entrance exams include sailing rough waters and gutting fish."

"I'm just saying"—Ash unfolded the tarp—"that particular weakness doesn't bode well for you being good at medicine, or even liking it. It seems probable that you wouldn't handle it well. Or you might end up thinking it a waste. I mean"— Ash wrinkled his nose like he'd put a piece of bad fish in his mouth— "we're talking about studying medicine. Sickness is gross. Sick people are gross."

Swift glanced back at the road leading up to town. He could just break for it.

But would Edric call that "running?"

Even if he would, coming here was turning out to be a mistake.

By confronting Ash, Swift was giving him an open chance to take clear shots.

Ash was obviously wanting to deepen the chasm between them, he on the side of success and adventure, with Swift left behind, watching him master a dream that they shared.

"Look, I'm happy for you," said Swift. "That's all I came to say."

"It feels great that you're happy for me."

Ash stared down the half inch he had on Swift.

"And you should be. Finding one of these old sea relics—it's like having the whole world delivered to you on a platter. Want to know how much money the Welsh museum wants to pay me?"

"Not really."

"Let's just say—I could buy my own boat. Imagine how much more of a reward the Star of Atlantis will land me."

Heat was building strongly in Swift's chest now. The next stage would be color flushing up his neck and into his face.

If that happened, Ash would know he was getting under Swift's skin.

Ash shook out the tarp. "Especially now that I'm well-known and certain to find it."

Swift could just walk away. They'd reached a place of Ash declaring that Swift was certain to fail at everything, while he himself was sure of a massive win.

At this point, bowing out couldn't be running. This confrontation was doing nothing to coax Ash to leave Swift alone.

And there was no chance Ash would betray anything.

But it didn't matter.

Swift had a lead that Ash knew nothing about.

He had the *Star of Atlantis* book and map.

And he now had a picture of Sterncastle Cove.

"You really don't have a clue what you're talking about." Swift glanced at the clouds, bluing deeply with rain. "I should go."

He backed off from Ash.

Turned away.

"I know why you really came down here," Ash called.

Swift stopped.

Ash set aside the tarp. "I know that you're jealous of me for going after the Star of Atlantis. I know that you're wanting a piece of my fame. There's no sense in hiding it."

"I..." Swift unzipped his jacket, letting in the cool wind. "I told you, I'm done with the Star of Atlantis."

"I know you better than that."

The devilish, handsome expression on Ash, showing such confidence, seemed part of the magic that made him so skilled at manipulation.

"You should give up your jealousy," said Ash. "You've never had much of a chance in this chase. Those old books of yours didn't help me. And after what I've discovered, I'd say you've got no chance."

Any lingering strength to stifle the building heat disappeared. Swift felt blown all the way open—his insecurities revealed and his heart at the ready for crushing.

"You don't know me." Swift moved in.

But of course Ash knew Swift. Deeply. He knew exactly how to offset Swift, how to lather him into exasperation and rivalry. This was his game, and at it he was winning.

Ash glanced at the storm-darkening sky as he climbed into the motorboat. "A few years ago, the Star of Atlantis was all you ever talked about." He hooked the tarp to the gunwale. "Psychotic obsessions like yours don't disappear. It makes me feel sorry for you."

Heat crept up Swift's neck.

He flipped up his collar, covering the red blotches that had to be growing visible. "Just because I'm interested in the Star of Atlantis—that doesn't mean I'm jealous of you. This Practicum—"

"Enough about the Practicum."

Ash jerked tight the cords on the tarp.

"Why are we even still talking about it?"

He hopped out of the boat.

"You think a medical Practicum is something special. But how many doctors do we really need? I bet there are a half dozen within shouting distance."

Ash rounded the boat, hooking the tarp as he went.

Swift stumbled back out of his way.

"And my father says doctors don't make that much money," said Ash. "Not once you consider all the debt and time they put in. I mean, I only needed one good lead to claim my treasure chest. A doctor has to invest a lifetime of grueling work. See what I mean about having 'the knack?'"

"If you believe slacking on research is the way to chase treasure, you'd better think again," said Swift. "It's a basic fact that what you get out of something is wholly dependent on what you put in."

"Ugh, you sound like a teacher."

Ash gave an easy laugh, like the two of them were old friends just casually chatting. Like they weren't knee deep in a full-on fight.

"Maybe lecturing is where you'll end up. That seems more your speed."

"You wouldn't know," said Swift. "You've never appreciated any teacher."

Ash seemed to be studying Swift's cheeks. He was certainly seeing the red blotches now.

Swift tried to think of a way to back out of this. Caius and Edric would certainly now tell him to get out of here. But to slow down, to drop this, felt like surrendering ground.

"Want to know what the very best part is about being a

winning treasure hunter?" asked Ash. "It's the way people look at me—with perfect admiration and respect. I don't have to listen to anyone anymore. It feels good...really good...to be recognized as gifted. To be called 'Devon's Brilliant Boy; Discoverer of Lost Treasure.'"

"If you really knew the value of discovering lost relics," said Swift, "you'd recognize that there's an intrinsic reward in sharing with others what you've found."

Ash studied Swift. "It really bothers you that I won't tell you what's in my treasure chest, huh."

"No. It doesn't."

"Maybe one day you'll understand why it's a good idea to keep these things private." He struggled against the wind as he strapped down the last bit of the tarp. "Even if you have no hope of finding the Star of Atlantis, perhaps you'll find a historic piece, someday. I always saw you doing something extraordinary."

"You don't think taking on a medical Practicum at our age is extraordinary?" asked Swift.

Ash shrugged. "Don't lots of people our age take on pointless Practicums?"

It was high time, now, to leave.

But Swift's feet wouldn't carry him away.

"And surely," said Ash, "you have to admit that doing a Practicum is nothing compared to discovering the Star of Atlantis."

His feet would only carry him closer to Ash.

Swift said—"What if you're not the only one planning to go after the Star of Atlantis?"

Ash flinched.

The words were out before Swift could think.

He shouldn't have said them. But seeing that shock on Ash's face felt so good.

Ash grinned. "I knew you couldn't handle your jealousy."

A heavy mist moved in—not rain quite yet, but it would build.

Ash focused hard on Swift. "It doesn't matter if you're going after the Star of Atlantis. Because I'll be the one to find it. And when I do, I'll forever be known as the Boy of Destiny. The Boy of Norse Pirate Secrets."

He came away from the boat, a hard wind driving behind him and bringing true rain.

"When I find the Star of Atlantis," said Ash, "my life will be endlessly interesting to everyone. The Star of Atlantis myth says it chooses its bearer. I mean to play that myth up. People will forever be asking me, 'Why did the Star of Atlantis fall into your hands?' They'll always be wondering what else I might try."

"The myth surrounding the Star of Atlantis is something to be handled carefully and examined," said Swift. "Just as much as the relic itself. It certainly isn't something to be used and milked, for ego and profit."

"If you buy those myths, you can't argue that point," said Ash. "If the Star of Atlantis 'chooses' me, doesn't that mean I can bloody well do what I want with it?"

"And what if it chooses me?" asked Swift, his voice raised.

Ash shrugged. "I guess we'll have to see what happens."

Swift wanted to holler that he'd found a map to the Star of Atlantis, that he was well on his way, that he had a lead to decipher. That despite what might be in that stupid Welsh box, Ash couldn't hold a candle to Swift's research.

And, if there was any destiny about this, a case could be made that the *Star of Atlantis* book and map had "chosen" Swift. They'd remained with him, even after Ash stole everything else.

But Swift managed to keep his mouth shut.

"I'm not so sure a person can have two dreams," said Ash. "I feel someone ought to caution you about that."

"You don't know anything about my dreams," said Swift. "You just got lucky with your find, and that's all. Do you actually think you could get lucky twice, after putting in so little work? At least I know the value of research. I know the value of leads."

The rain was pelting hard now, but Ash seemed to not even notice.

"You can't actually think you have some lead to where the Star of Atlantis is," said Ash.

Swift felt like a sail, out of control and whipping in the wind. "I might have an idea or two."

Ash scoffed. "I doubt you're capable of that."

Swift's face felt so hot that the rain seemed to sizzle. "I found a picture," he said, almost shouting. "A picture of what Sterncastle Cove actually looks like."

"Sterncastle Cove," Ash repeated. "You think the Star of Atlantis is in a place called Sterncastle Cove?"

Swift stood stunned, unable to process that he'd let those words escape.

Ash seemed to relax. Seemed relieved. Satisfied. Like he'd been the one waiting for Swift to give up something valuable.

And he had.

Swift composed his face as well as he could; tried to manage a shaking that'd come into his throat. "The reason I really came down here was to say, best of luck to you. Because I'm going after the Star of Atlantis, same as you."

"Thanks for the heads up." Ash started up the beach, toward the cobbled road leading to their neighborhood. "I've got to run. I have some planning to do."

Despite the driving rain, Swift couldn't move. Despite its chill, he was bathing in heat.

He'd betrayed his hard-won lead. Even though, by weeks of agonizing work, he'd earned it, it belonged to Ash now.

It seemed that even this storm belonged to Ash. And with it, he'd bound Swift to remain far behind him.

7

The instant Ash was out of sight, Swift sank to a crouch. He'd just blabbed a half dozen things that should've remained unsaid. Tears didn't visit him often, but he couldn't contain his frustration at his own incompetence in handling Ash. He couldn't believe he'd surrendered a lead to the Star of Atlantis.

It was nothing for Ash to demolish Swift's confidence, to goad him into a defensive state, to strip away what he'd worked for.

Swift wiped at his face, piping hot and dripping with rain. Why was it so easy to fumble into Ash's traps?

"Swift? Is that you?"

Swift glanced up to see Edric jogging over from a seaside pub, holding his jacket over his head to fend off the downpour.

"What in the world are you doing on this soppy beach in the middle of all this rain?" He drew Swift under his jacket. "You'll get sick is the thing. You can bet Caius won't take you sailing this weekend if you've got a cold."

Swift could barely make his way to his feet, could barely see for the heat in his face. "We're not going sailing."

Edric steadied him. "What do you mean, you're not going sailing?"

Swift kicked sand toward Ash's boat. "We're going to kick some ass."

"Lord, you just talked to Ash, didn't you?" Edric hustled him up the road leading back to town. "I hope you told him all about your Practicum, and where he can stick that damn box."

Swift rubbed water out of his eyes, off his cheeks.

"You're not crying," said Edric. "Are you?"

The fury was so strangling, Swift found he couldn't even look at Edric, much less respond.

Edric guided him under the awning of a coffee shop. "We'll just wait here a moment, until the rain lets up."

Swift took a deep breath. "It's the rain. I'm not crying."

"Sit down." Edric moved him to a small bistro table. He wrung out his jacket and hung it on the back of a chair. "What did the little twerp say?"

Swift had to clench his hands to keep them from shaking. "He said that I have no chance of finding the Star of Atlantis. He said that he's certain that he'll hunt it down with no effort. That he has 'the knack.'"

Edric flagged down a waitress. "Can you bring something warm for him? Hot cocoa?"

Swift glanced up at Edric. "He said that I have a weak stomach because he's seen me seasick. He talked about how I can't gut a fish."

"Okay—a weak stomach. A struggle with blood. Was he talking about sailing, or medicine?"

Swift stared at his hands, hot and clammy. "He thinks the Practicum is worthless."

"So, let me get this straight. Ash pummeled you into this state of frantic competition, this desperation to beat him to the Star of Atlantis, while casting doubt about whether you can make it into the Practicum?"

Swift focused on the burn in his hands. "I can't let him get away with this. I won't let him shake my confidence."

"But you did let him shake you," said Edric. "The way you feel right now—this is exactly what Ash wanted. He casts lies to bait you, and you snap them right up. If you ask me, you lost this bout."

"Well I won't lose the next one. Every word he said made me want to find the Star of Atlantis and smear the asphalt with him."

"Ash has got you pinned," said Edric, "but with nothing more than a tack. You can be free of him if you want. But it's all up to you."

Swift rubbed at the back of his neck. "He's done this to me over and over. He's blamed me for our crumbling friendship when it was he who cast me off. When it was he who stole my books. And now he seems to recognize that I want the Practicum as badly as I've wanted any treasure. And so he's throwing me off it."

"So, this time—don't let him."

"You can bet I won't let him," said Swift. "I'll show him I can find the Star of Atlantis. I'll show him I can do anything I set my mind to."

"You mean, you can do anything *he* sets your mind to."

"That's not fair."

"It's bullseye," said Edric, "and you know it."

Edric was right that Ash had manipulated him. That Ash always managed to manipulate him. But Edric was dead wrong if he thought the only reason Swift wanted to chase the Star of Atlantis was because of Ash's provocation.

"Finding treasure was my dream long before it was his," said Swift. "I have to find the Star of Atlantis."

Edric drew his gaze. "You really don't."

"If I don't, it'll mean that the most significant treasure in maritime legends will end up in the hands of that selfish blowhole."

"If the Star of Atlantis were findable, maybe," said Edric.

"I have a lead." Swift squeezed shut his eyes. "But—I was so flustered and angry, and Ash wouldn't stop goading me, and"— he glanced away from Edric—"I let it slip."

Edric handed him a napkin. "Wipe that rain off your face."

"It was my lead. I earned it." Swift buried his face in the napkin. "And I just handed it right to Ash."

"What kind of lead is it?"

"A woodblock print," said Swift. "An actual image of Sterncastle Cove. I found it in an old microfiche archive, and it correlates perfectly to the cove on my map." He dropped against the back of his chair. "I shouted at Ash that I'd discovered that picture."

"Is that all you told him? That you saw a picture?"

"Yes, but—it's worse than that," said Swift. "Ash had no idea that the Star of Atlantis is said to be stowed in a place called Sterncastle Cove. Now that he knows, he might find where it is and reach it before I can."

"Ash isn't going to reach it." Edric received the hot cocoa from the waitress and set it before Swift.

Swift leaned over the mug. Let its steam bathe his cheeks. "How can you be so sure?"

"Well, setting aside my skepticism that the Star of Atlantis even exists, knowing the name of an alleged cove won't help Ash. From what you've told me, Sterncastle Cove isn't mentioned anyplace, really. Except in the book you possess, and now on that block print you found. And it's not like you showed Ash the picture, right?"

"That's true."

Swift ran his finger around the rim of his mug.

And it was also true that Ash was terrible at research. If he were to give the idea just a glance, he'd find nothing.

"Maybe he'll think I made the whole thing up to throw him off." Swift sat up a little straighter. "Even if he managed, somehow, to dig up the same picture, it isn't explicit at all—it needs interpretation. He could never manage that." He focused on Edric. "But I can."

"Hang on, don't get too excited."

Edric fixed the steaming mug inside Swift's hands.

"One blocky print of what someone a few hundred years ago thought Sterncastle Cove looked like isn't much for you to go off of either."

The mug was scalding, but the pain felt good. It was a match to the heat in Swift, an energy stirring up ideas on how he could tackle that block print.

"Even so, it's true that there's no other research to be had." Swift watched the froth in his mug take the shape of a sea eddy. "Ash claimed that he has a lead, too, from whatever rubbish was in his treasure chest. But he certainly might've been lying. And there's something true-seeming about my woodblock print."

"True-*seeming*?"

Swift met Edric's stare.

"The idea needs work, I know. But besides the cryptic stuff written in my book, on my map, that picture is the only descriptive bit I've dredged up. And believe me—my research is solid."

Edric leaned his elbows on the table. "Let's set aside your thoughts of the chase for a minute. As much of an achievement as finding the Star of Atlantis would be, think about the work you'll do, trying to test into the Practicum. It'll be worlds harder. That's worth some respect, even trying—even if you don't make it in."

"It's not enough to just try." Swift stood. "Ash said that trying was all that mattered because there's no way I could ever get in. What if he's right?"

Edric took him by the arm and eased him back to sitting. "If you let yourself be dizzied and manipulated so easily, you won't stand any chance at success. Not with the Practicum, and not with any treasure chase."

"I'm going after the Star of Atlantis," said Swift. "And for my own reasons. I'll come through with a sound strategy."

"Have your adventure, then."

Edric leaned back.

"And I hope that you find what you're looking for. But believe me, lad—even finding the Star of Atlantis isn't going to resolve this petty war you're allowing with Ash."

"Yes, it would. Finding the Star of Atlantis would solve everything. Why can't you see that?"

Edric's expression took on a thoughtful tone. "Think back to that day, five or six years ago, when you crashed your go-cart, racing Ash."

"What's that got to do with anything? That was an accident."

"It was no accident. Mr. Emberly warned Ash to avoid that part of the track, that there was an oil slick. Ash thought it sounded fun to try riding it, but Mr. Emberly talked him out of it. So what did Ash do? Do you even remember?"

"He raced me," said Swift. "He braked before the slick, and I rode into it."

"And smashed up the cart, and your ribs. While he watched. While he laughed."

"I only was bruised up," said Swift. "I didn't break anything."

Saying the words, Swift realized they belonged to Ash. This was what Ash said anytime they'd talked about it.

"Only bruised up." Edric's expression darkened.

He wasn't just annoyed with Ash. On Edric's face rested a cold, controlled fury. If Ash happened by, it seemed Edric might very well tear his arms off.

Reading that fury on Edric—a fury directed at someone who'd hurt his brother—Swift felt a rare comfort.

It dawned on him that this is what Edric's caring felt like. Protection. Edric wanted to protect him.

Or, more—Edric wanted Swift to learn how to protect himself.

And seeing through Edric's eyes, through Edric's anger, Swift could read Ash in a way that he hadn't before.

It was petty of Ash to press him into competing. But it was downright vicious of him to mess with Swift's confidence.

Swift lowered his gaze to his lap. "I let him get to me." He rubbed his eyes. "I truly let him get to me."

Edric drew Swift's hands down. "When I see you on Monday—when you're back from your adventure with Caius—don't expect any disappointment from me that your hands are empty. And I'll expect to see no disappointment on you, either. Instead, I'd like to see a lad who can finally move on."

"If I come back empty-handed, I know you wouldn't think less of me," said Swift. "Caius wouldn't think less of me."

Edric captured his glance. "And neither will Justus."

But Ash had spoken of Justus—Justus admiring Ash for his discovery. What if that were true?

"It's just," said Swift, "I don't want the Practicum to be a next-best thing."

"It's a deuced medical Practicum you'd be taking on at fourteen. How could that be second to anything?" Edric shook out his jacket and laid it in a patch of sunlight, spreading with the storm's dissolution.

The sun's intermittence, breaking the thinning clouds, shone through the crystal-clear air left by the passing of rain. Through the shattered sky, sunbeams glittered on the cobbled street, beams swelling nearer like a rising tide.

One day was all Swift had left before the sailing trip. One day to decipher his meager leads and form a plan to discover the Star of Atlantis.

Claiming that treasure would mean rescuing it from Ash. It would mean poaching from Ash his foregone conclusion that the treasure all but belonged to him.

And finding the Star of Atlantis would mean more than that he'd simply outwitted, outraced Ash.

By finding the Star of Atlantis, Swift would be making good on his faith in himself—faith that he truly could reach his dreams.

"The Star of Atlantis may not seem as important as the Practicum." Swift lifted his gaze to meet Edric's. "But somehow, it is. My heart tells me it is. I have to find the Star of Atlantis."

"Follow your heart, then," said Edric, leaning in. "Go after that bloody dream—everyone else be damned. And after your fever of the Star of Atlantis breaks, promise me that you'll set yourself down to work even more doggedly at a dream that's truer to who you actually are."

"Compared with what Ash has accomplished," said Swift, "even the study of medicine feels small." He met Edric's gaze. "That ends this weekend."

Edric rested back. "That's my lad."

8

Shards of rain pelted Justus' study window.

Swift sat, deliciously dwarfed, behind his father's oak desk, sorrel red like the coat of a stallion.

It was the night before his treasure chase with Caius, and before him rose towers of heavy books that he'd dredged up over the past weeks, on the maritime history of Wales.

In none of them was the Star of Atlantis described.

It might just be a plain artifact from everyday life—more novelty than valuable—not worth mentioning.

But. It might be a glut of wealth stowed inside a treasure chest.

Or an Egyptian queen's lost jewel.

Or a key to unlocking some ancient secret.

Swift peered through the stacks of books and watched rain lash the bay window.

The glass looked thick and heavy, the way all of Justus' things looked heavy—his cluttered collections of medical books, his large-eyed telescope peering into the storm, the cart of crystal-corked bourbon and scotch bottles, the dark leather armchair, high-backed, worn with the heavy use of a father who'd taught four sons a love for reading.

On the wall, over the reading chair, display lights shone on an oil painting of their great *Regulus Borealis* brigantine ship.

And before the painting hung an iron chandelier with bulbs shaped like dripping candles, its metal shuddering with rumbles of close thunder.

All this weight, this deep wood, this rain, created a sense of being a notorious pirate himself; of sitting in a captain's lair on some lavish Norse ship that governors feared, its wheel pried from the hand of a powerful king, its brig full of people who'd wronged him, its steerage full of jewels.

The blue of Swift's laptop, glowing at the epicenter of the books, shed a light too artificial, too glaring for the antiquated mood of the room. But it was worth it.

After pouring over obscure websites for days, Swift finally had stumbled on a geology site showing remarkably accurate illustrations of the northern coastline of Pembrokeshire in Wales, fringing the great Wentletrap Forest.

They were like Sibley's drawings of birds—the illustrations more true, more helpful to identification, than even a picture might be.

Though a small find, though not definitive, two coves stood out as prime candidates for exploration. Both seemed to match the description from his Star of Atlantis book and map, and both seemed true to the only portrayal he'd found that allegedly was of Sterncastle Cove—the woodblock print.

The woodblock print was black-inked and simple, done from the perspective of someone watching from a ship over-looking Sterncastle Cove—splashy in the throes of a turbulent sea.

Swift rambled through the geology website a final time, noting the coordinates of the two coves, scribbling down what he could deduce about their best access points, about the natures of those waters in autumn.

He noted the fish and the sharks and the coastal plants and animals that might be sighted, lurking around their rocks; the shore birds that might be circling.

Staring at the woodblock print, Swift could lose himself,

imagining gliding into Sterncastle Cove like old Grog Blossom had on the deep night when he stowed the Star of Atlantis.

Though nothing in any of the books came close to revealing where the Star of Atlantis might rest, Swift had discovered a detailed history of how it'd been lost at the hand of old Grog Blossom—a notorious Norse pirate who turned out to be more hero than villain.

Grog Blossom was actually a historical figure—a corsair pirate who captained a ship called the Checkered Whelk. Records of his ship appeared in several places, a fact which—along with the plentiful tales of his deeds—seemed to heighten the legitimacy of the legends surrounding the Star of Atlantis.

Grog Blossom was born under the name Cynfael Maddox, and his crew included other Norse pirates of the age.

But Maddox and his crew weren't pirates in the traditional sense. They dealt in things more precious than treasures and wealth. They robbed from oppressors and distributed the goods among neglected villages. Maddox had a fondness for sharing books, and with them the talents of reading and writing.

Some of the records of Cynfael Maddox were search warrants issued by the tyrants he'd plundered. Others were tales written by grateful villagers, able not just to survive, but to thrive because of the bounties he won.

Some called him a "renaissance man," and others a "renaissance maker," his gifts lifting people not just out of poverty but into enlightenment. Key art works and literature created in that age came from commoners inspired by the books and the knowledge he'd bring, along with the wealth.

The most noteworthy treasure that Maddox filched was said to be the Star of Atlantis.

Though the account described nothing of what the Star of Atlantis was, it did say that Maddox plundered it from a King's treasury of crown jewels, lending it the ring of great wealth.

The king set sail in a rage when he discovered his Star had been lost. He seized Cynfael Maddox and sentenced him to death, but not before Maddox had hidden the Star of Atlantis.

Fantastical rumors spread that that King not only dealt

death by poison and steel to the crew of the Checkered Whelk, but that he paid a sorcerer to lay on Maddox a curse.

No peace would come to the thief, in life or in death, until he returned the Star of Atlantis to the King's waiting hand.

But Maddox never did.

And so seafarers, for centuries following, reported seeing a mystical light on the water, or hearing a ghostly voice ring from the wilderness of the sea, or sighting an empty vessel, cruising full sailed, near the Welsh coast.

They attributed the eerie disturbances to Cynfael Maddox's mutinous ghost, living on in aggravation, in death, ever defying the tyrant who destroyed his life and his crew.

But more fascinating than ghost tales, even, were the accounts less outlandish, for they were certainly closer to the truth.

The more grounded accounts claimed that the King did pursue Maddox but failed to kill him. Rather, he only managed to break up the Checkered Whelk's crew, murdering some and banishing others.

And so Maddox and the other survivors faded into obscurity among the isles, keeping silent their secret of where the Star of Atlantis was stowed, taking shelter and protection from villages to whom they'd been kind.

And a wild version, prolific in these records Swift had dredged up, rang slightly familiar to him. This might mean he'd once read the version in a book Ash now had.

But he couldn't be sure.

This wild version of Cynfael Maddox's tale claimed that he and his crew were some kind of guru immortals, or perhaps the mortal offspring of an ancient, nearly god-like clan that sought to harbor wisdom and live at peace. To protect what they held sacred—maybe treasures, maybe nature, maybe culture, maybe their ancient Welsh lands and seas.

These ancient people were known as the Shepherds of the Stars, and all the records referencing them agreed that Cynfael Maddox was known to be of that tradition.

Swift set aside the book of the account and picked up his

notes. He was just settling into adding more details when a terrific burst of thunder pealed.

A flash of lightning lashed the yard just meters from the study window. The computer shorted and snapped off.

The room went black as trench waters.

His ears ringing, his face flush from the heat of the strike, Swift stumbled to the window.

Outside, flames were licking the trunk of an ancient oak tree, huge and sprawling—the best climbing tree in their grove.

The rearing flames tore at its branches and went at the heartwood, making even the trunk glow a hellish red.

Flames rose until a torrent of storm gushed, dousing them, leaving just an orange core simmering inside the oak's battered branches.

Swift startled at the door creaking open.

"Swift?" It was Caius.

At the sound of his voice, the tension from the fright eased.

As far back as Swift could remember—all the way to when he was barely more than a baby—when he was frightened, he called out for Caius.

"Here," whispered Swift.

"You all right?"

Swift tripped over a stack of books.

"Don't move," said Caius. "I'll find you."

Caius stumbled through the dark until he touched Swift's shoulder. He guided him away from the window and to the clearer middle of the room.

They together watched the storm rage, the tree smolder.

The sky's manic flashings showed gray smoke and cinders pouring from the struck limbs.

The best climber of the Kingsley boys, Swift had squirreled up that ancient oak daily in summers, reading from its loft, falling out of it from time to time.

Caius claimed that the lion's share of his interest in medicine had come from patching Swift—wrapping sprains, binding cuts, and even, once he started his training, stitching Swift's shoulder after a daring jump out of that tree. The sight of it burning was sheer tragedy. The dark smoke funereal.

That tree had been almost like a brother.

Swift tightened his grip on Caius' arm, crossing his chest. "Are Mum and Justus all right?"

"They're upstairs. No electricity there, either. Stay put, I'll find a torch." He left Swift in the middle of the room.

"Don't we need to go see about the tree?" asked Swift.

"I'm sorry, but the tree's gone," said Caius. "There's nothing we can do."

"What if the storm doesn't put out the flames? What if they spread, and the house catches fire?"

"That won't happen in all this wet. Stay where you are. I'll see if I can get the power going."

Standing in the middle of the study—utterly black but for lightning-bright rain smattering the glass, the darkness broken by cackles of thunder—Swift absolutely felt he was standing in a pirate's cabin, atop a rollicking sea.

When Swift was younger, when nights this black swallowed him, his imagination would've gotten the better of him, and he would've suffered night terrors.

But grown more now—on the verge of fourteen—he could comprehend how Caius seemed always unafraid. Always hopeful. And he found he could mirror that.

Still, though, the terror from the lightning bursts tingled in his belly and was making his heart a jackrabbit.

But he wished the storm would keep up all night. What used to be fear now tasted of delicious adrenaline, like what had coursed through him on the black morning when Justus chased after him on the gray-misted sea, pretending to be old undead Grog Blossom.

"I think I might've found Sterncastle Cove," Swift whispered to the darkness.

"Nice work," the darkness returned. "Is it far?"

"I'm not exactly sure. I've narrowed it down to two coves that, from aerial pictures, both look right. I believe it's named Sterncastle Cove for a reason—inside both coves are high islets.

They're big enough for holding a cavern, sort of like captain's quarters beneath the sterncastle on a ship."

"Are they off the coast of Pembrokeshire, like you imagined they'd be?"

Caius was speaking in a hushed tone, as Swift was, as any sensible person would, to keep the mood of the blackout electric.

"Yes," Swift whispered back. "I think they're not far from our beach house. They both edge the Wentletrap Forest. And I discovered some wonderful Star of Atlantis lore. Old Grog Blossom—he was an actual person. His real name was Cynfael Maddox."

"How about that," said Caius.

"He was a corsair pirate who captained a ship called the Checkered Whelk. His crew included other notorious pirates— Chance Merriweather, and Griselda Jib, and Bones Cooper, and others. They plundered kings and wealthy freights and spread their bounty to the poor. Every coastal city in Europe cheered at the coming of his flag."

"That's more detail than you imagined you'd find, I think," whispered Caius.

"It turns out, Maddox stole the Star of Atlantis from a tyrannical king's ship, beneath the tyrannical king's very eye, from his treasury of crown jewels. Some say the king captured and poisoned Maddox. Others say the King banished him. But not before the old bootlegger managed to stash the Star of Atlantis."

Drawers creaked as Caius poked around the edges of the study for a light.

"The accounts claiming Maddox was murdered say that the king cursed him to sail the seas as old Grog Blossom, day and night, in death, until he recovered the Star of Atlantis and returned it to the king's hoard. But Cynfael Maddox, even cursed in death, couldn't be bound to obey the tyrant. So instead, he set his sails to guard the Star of Atlantis from greedy hearts. And he haunts the seas even to this day."

"Sounds like a real Robin Hood," said Caius. "I like those sorts of fantasies."

"The true account, though, is more fascinating than even that fantasy."

"Oh?" Caius seemed to be digging in a trunk.

"These accounts claim that something terrible happened that brought Cynfael Maddox and his crew to destitution. The rulers they plundered eventually took revenge, catching and killing some of the Checkered Whelk's crew. So they disbanded. But some say the remnants of that crew still linger. Whether as ghosts or as some kind of guru immortals, or descendants of an old clan called the Shepherds of the Stars, they're said to keep to the wilds of the Welsh coast, gathering wisdom and seeking to teach and living off the land on the dregs of whatever treasures they yet possess. Maybe the Star of Atlantis."

A light flashed in the corner of the room.

Caius stood from kneeling.

He closed the lid to the trunk he'd pillaged and went to a breaker box in the study's corner.

The light Caius held was just a battery-powered one, but it was made to look like an old-fashioned lantern. Perfect.

"Looks like the storm's punched out everything," said Caius. "There won't be any power until the grid's reset. I bet the whole village is out."

"If the power doesn't come back soon," said Swift, "we'll run out of freshwater. We'll have to break for land, despite the storm —despite the kraken—if we're to survive."

Caius shed a small laugh. "And what ship are we on this time?"

"It'd better be the Checkered Whelk," said Swift. "Best we pay our respects to Norse pirates, if we're to go plundering their treasures."

Caius closed the breaker box. "Let's have a look at the coves you've found."

Swift took the light from him and led him to their father's desk. "I jotted down the coordinates of those two best ones, but I haven't looked them up yet to locate precisely where they are." He handed Caius his notes. "And the woodblock print—it's believed to actually be a rendition of Sterncastle Cove. I think it might help us figure out which of those two coves is more likely the right one."

Swift showed him the picture he'd taken of the microfiche film. The picture of Sterncastle Cove.

Caius angled the picture. "I'm afraid this print might not be that much help, really. It looks like every cove I've ever seen."

"I know," said Swift. "Except for this." He brought nearer the light and pointed to the edge of the picture. "The artist took the time to include birds swarming over the water."

Caius glanced at him. "What do you make of that?"

"I noticed a similar scavenger swarm when we were sailing this summer. The cove with the swarm I saw couldn't be Sterncastle Cove—the shape's all wrong. But it made me consider what could be dead there, and why. This picture looks like birds feeding on carrion, just like what I saw."

"So—you think Sterncastle Cove tends to collect carrion?" asked Caius.

"Maybe some coves are more treacherous than others—not just to ships, but to sea creatures, too. Maybe Sterncastle Cove is riddled with danger. My more-reasonable interpretation is that schools of sharks lurk in Sterncastle Cove, attracted by all the blood that would slosh around in the tides when ships and fish are dashed on its rocks. In a cove like that, there'd always be a cyclone of hunting birds."

Caius lifted a brow. "And let's hear your less-reasonable interpretation."

"Mermaids."

Swift bent closer to the picture.

"Mermaids might infest those waters, dragging their kill down to appease their goddess. If mermaids gathered there, swarms of birds would certainly be on hand to pick the bones of their slaughters."

Caius studied Swift's notes, his finger finding an estimation of the coordinates on a map. "Mermaid myths aside, you've got a sharp plan."

"So, I'm thinking we should sail to the coordinates of these two coves and favor the one with heavier swarms of birds."

Swift slid his Star of Atlantis book from his pocket. He opened it to the verse describing Sterncastle Cove.

Caius leaned in and read out loud—

"When the shore draws long and straight, skim the briny banks. Be swallowed by Sterncastle Cove. Seek the islet, round as Earth, studded with Kraken fangs. Mind the deeps for mermaid tails, shimmering blue and green. Heed their song, but touch the water not, lest your life be forfeit to their goddess. Always keep a weather eye on the mist coiling in the cove, for through it paddles old Grog Blossom, always dead, yet ever awake, cursed to forever sail as watchman over the Star of Atlantis."

"Grog Blossom." Caius smiled. "I've never seen Justus laugh harder than he did that morning."

"Yes, and who knows? Cynfael Maddox might really be out there. Maybe as a phantom pirate, maybe as a guru immortal."

Caius trailed his fingers down the side of the page, over a line of sketched water monsters: dazzle-tailed mermaids, the rage-eyed Cthulhu, the hungry Beisht Kione, a Rusalka maiden, gripping a knife, a skeletal pirate sailing a longboat.

"I've always wondered whether sea monsters and pirate ghosts weren't conjured by sailors, truly in danger, deathly afraid," said Caius. "I wonder if they're not an imaginative mind's manifestations of the actual terrors of the sea."

Swift settled against the bay window seat behind the desk. "What terrors of the sea could be more horrifying than blood-thirsty mermaids, or the Cthulhu, or the bone-crushing Kraken?"

"What about actual drowning?" Caius sat down, too, balancing the lantern between them. "Drowning people certainly would feel like they were slipping into the belly of a beast. Or how about running out of food or water on the sea? Just imagine the terror of knowing you're about to die, in the worst way, and yet being unable to do a thing about it. Wouldn't you feel like you were inside the jaws of the Cthulhu?"

"I guess. But I'd still rather believe there are actual Krakens," said Swift. "I like the idea of mermaids haunting waters, twisting the minds of sailors with their singing, so the sailors will draw close, and so they'll slip into the sea and drown themselves for the sake of beauty."

Caius eyed him sidelong. "You don't really believe that you saw a mermaid the night you took the *Strider*, before Justus caught you."

Swift released his gaze from Caius' smirk. "I can't make sense of what I saw. It couldn't have been a shark. It was long, shaped kind of like a fish's tail. It shone."

"Okay but please tell me you don't really believe mermaids were out there."

"Welsh Fishermen say there are mermaids," said Swift.

"Welsh Fishermen like to drink ale."

Swift looked Caius in the eye. "There absolutely was something in the water that night—shimmery blue and way down in the depths. Mermaids make for a working explanation."

"So do bioluminescent fauna or algae."

"Maybe. But I'm not convinced we should rule out mermaids."

Caius tapped Swift's page of coordinates. "I suppose you'll find out this weekend."

Swift took the page and studied it.

"The Star of Atlantis might be out there, Caius, just waiting for us. If it is, could you even imagine? There couldn't be a better fourteenth birthday."

Caius stood. "Do you feel ready to sail the *Regulus* this distance, just the two of us? It'll be a lot of work."

"And a lot of fun. When we come back, we might be heroes. Famous. Pirates!"

Caius lifted Swift's Star of Atlantis book. "Unless we come back maimed from all those monsters."

Swift marked the description of Sterncastle Cove with the page of coordinates. "Especially if we come back maimed from all those monsters."

9

The day of the treasure hunt, Caius and Swift drove to Ilfracombe. Here, Justus kept the *Regulus* and the *Strider* together docked.

A stop at the tavern on the wharf had become a tradition before setting out, and just as the sun was rising, they settled into a booth for a full English breakfast.

As the waitress laid down their plates, the tavern door swung.

"Good God—you were serious!" came a voice from across the tavern.

"I don't believe it." Swift laid down his fork.

Caius turned.

Ash strode through the tavern right to them. "I heard you were setting out today."

The waitress came by with a water glass. "Will you be joining them?"

Swift shook his head.

"Thank you." Ash took the glass and slid in beside Caius.

"You came here—to Ilfracombe—just to see if we were setting out?" asked Caius.

"As it happens," said Ash, "I myself am setting out today.

The wind beckons, the sea calls, and the Star of Atlantis awaits."

Caius cast an odd look at Ash. "Your father's motorboat docks in Clovelly."

"That's true." Ash scooped a spoonful of beans from Swift's plate. "But I've hired a professional sailing crew, based out of Ilfracombe. You can do that sort of thing once you've found something valuable and have what my father calls 'a stash to invest.'"

"Who told you we were setting out?" asked Swift.

"I've been rummaging through the same libraries you hit." Ash shrugged. "People talk."

"Not to be rude," said Swift, "but Caius and I were looking forward to some time on our own."

"I get it," said Ash. "I'll leave in a sec. But before I do, I thought I might offer you a tip."

"A tip."

Swift stared at him.

"You want to offer us a tip."

"I know you," said Ash. "I know how you think. I promise—you're going to set out the wrong way."

"If we're both chasing the Star of Atlantis, why would you care to help me?" asked Swift.

"Call it being a good sport," said Ash. "Once I find the Star, it'll be great to get to tell reporters that I had competition. That I did what I could to help them along."

Whatever this was, it wasn't being a good sport.

Clearly, he wanted to manipulate Swift into giving something else up.

Ash leaned back casually, stretching out one arm along the back of the booth behind Caius. "So—where are you thinking Sterncastle Cove is?"

Swift glanced down at his plate, half-picked off.

He studied Ash—seeming to want to cast the impression that he was a part of Swift's brotherhood with Caius.

"You can't imagine I'm going to tell you our strategy."

"What, do you not want to hear what I have to say?" asked Ash.

"I don't recall asking you for help."

"You might as well tell me something," said Ash. "I mean, I'm right here, aren't I? I'll see you set off, and there's nothing you can do about it."

"So—you mean to follow us," said Caius.

Swift crumpled his napkin.

"I'm not going to follow you," said Ash. "Doing so would be foolish. I'm certain you've charted the course all wrong. I, on the other hand, have figured it out."

Swift studied Ash, cool as ever.

Was all this meant to be a distraction? Ash trying to get inside Swift's head. Or could he possibly know something legitimate? Whatever he was meaning by this, he was certainly draining out the fun.

Swift glanced at Caius' car outside. They could just go home. They could leave Ash with no inkling of their plans.

It would feel good to drive off, intending to come back, more covertly, another time. It would feel good to watch Ash diminish, aimless on the water with just his professional sailors and his boasts (likely empty) that he had a solid destination.

But there was no other time. This was it—Swift's only opportunity to go after the Star of Atlantis. His last chance.

"You have in mind to travel someplace up north, don't you?" asked Ash.

The only way Ash could've figured that out is if he coerced the librarian to pull the very same articles he'd pulled for Swift.

"Maybe—to the northern shores of Pembrokeshire?" asked Ash.

Swift didn't respond.

"I knew it." Ash settled back. Stretching his arm more closely around Caius.

Caius eyed Ash's hand on his shoulder.

"The thing is," said Ash, "lots of people have looked for the treasure up north, along coasts edging the Wentletrap. And nobody's found it. Doesn't that tell you something? I, on the other hand, have thought to look where no one else has. My research has guided me to a much more likely trove."

"And where would that be?" asked Swift.

Ash grinned. "In your Mum's—."

"That's plenty." Caius herded Ash, cackling, out of the booth.

"No, but seriously." Ash leaned his hands on the table. "Sterncastle Cove isn't north. If you're smart, you'll listen to me and not go to the trouble of scavenging places that've been turned over a thousand times."

Swift tried to conceal the smile that was forming on his face.

Ash had tried to press Swift into betraying his destination. But Ash was the one giving up something this time.

Ash's research had to be terrible.

The truth was that the coves along Pembrokeshire's northern reaches hadn't been investigated that much. Most of the searching had been along its far western edge.

There were new kinds of algae and coral and fish in those northern coves, still being identified, slowly, the islets and coastal caverns off their shores being so complex to get to.

And a key point—not only were those northern Pembrokeshire coasts as remote and unsettled as they had been for hundreds of years, but, as famed as the Star of Atlantis was in sea lore, not that many people were known to have methodically tried to find it.

Swift stood from their booth. "Thanks for the tip." He glanced at the door.

"You'd be wise to listen to me," said Ash, backing off. "The southern coast of Wales is unhunted. That's the jackpot. That's where I'm going. And that's where you should go, too. Especially if you've only got one weekend left."

Caius stood, too. "I think it's time you were on your way."

Ash, eyeing Swift, left the tavern.

Swift and Caius eased back into their booth.

Swift stared at the front door, closing slowly behind Ash. "What was that?"

"That was a perfect of example of a guy with zero life."

Caius took the ticket from the waitress. "He's in your head, and he knows it. He's only trying to stay there."

"To have come after us like that, though. To have followed us here. It feels like he meant to do more than just mess with me."

"Don't you think he wants to throw you off the chase? Like ever, he's after depleting you," said Caius. "Maddening you so that you might trip up."

"When I was researching, I did tell a librarian that you and I were sailing this weekend." Swift pushed away his plate. "He must've told Ash everything. Showed him all the articles I opened."

Caius glanced behind him at the door of the tavern. "If Ash knew our strategy, he wouldn't have come after you like this. He would've just used it to gain an edge."

"That might be right. But—"

"Look, we know he likes to take things from you and run. And anyway, you've put in weeks of work—as much of it at home as at the library. We know Ash well enough to be confident he hasn't done squat."

Swift scanned the blue line of sea leading to the south coast of Wales.

It was true that no documented scouting for the Star of Atlantis had ever been done there.

"What if Ash did do some research?" asked Swift. "Or what if his treasure chest rubbish pointed him to the south side of Wales? He knows I wouldn't listen to him. He might've just told me exactly where he thinks Sterncastle Cove is, precisely so I wouldn't go looking that way."

"You still can't see it, can you?" Caius picked up his jacket. "His only aim is to make you doubt yourself. You've done your research, right? And it's strong. As Edric would say—don't take the bait."

Of course the best thing Swift could do was ignore Ash. But any sense of self-doubt, once laid by Ash, felt indivisible from Swift's body. It was like a layer of sweat—something he couldn't just shake.

"I have skepticism about my own ideas," said Swift. "Every researcher should. My theories aren't conclusive—"

"If Ash could see the doubt coming into your face, he'd be loving it. Don't give him that." Caius gestured toward the door. "Let's get out of here. The wind will be picking up about now."

Swift lifted his jacket and followed Caius to the door but—

Ash was still there, right outside, talking to three big guys—his professional sailors, probably.

Swift held Caius back.

"Ash isn't even dressed right for sailing," Swift whispered. "Do you think he really believes he has a shot at finding the Star of Atlantis? Or does he not even think that it's possible? Some part of me wonders if treasure hunting for him is nothing more than a show."

"You might be on it," said Caius. "If that's how he operates, then of course he'll get nowhere."

Swift carefully watched Ash, seeming so clever, standing so confidently, speaking to the three rugged sailors, all of them studying the sea.

If Ash truly believed that the Star of Atlantis was a complete myth, that there was nothing to be had except hype—it was logical that he'd play that up.

"What if the Star of Atlantis isn't out there?" Swift gazed at Ash, the blue of the water glancing smartly off his sunglasses. "What if no one has any shot of finding the Star of Atlantis?"

Caius fixed on him. "Do you think the Star of Atlantis is out there?"

It was a bare fact that a mythology had accreted around the Star of Atlantis, like a stalagmite grown over a long span of time. It'd always struck Swift as impossible that so many tales could gather around an artifact that was wholly fictional.

And many of the clues to where it might rest were scientifically based.

The Star of Atlantis was a marvel, certainly, and beyond-belief-cool. Impossible seeming. But—was the whole world, in its essence, not a thing beyond belief?

Swift met Caius' gaze. "The Star of Atlantis..."

The Star of Atlantis—a treasure that deepened the mystery of the sea that he loved.

The Star of Atlantis—an emblem of his childhood and a symbol of how he could gain distance from that childhood and finally reach confidence.

Conquest.

"...it has to be out there."

10

Swift and Caius watched from inside the tavern as Ash spoke with his three sailors—

"How are we going to get our gear?" asked Swift. "How will we reach the *Regulus*?"

Caius whispered, "We'll have to dodge him. Think we're clever enough?"

Swift stifled a laugh.

One of the sailors seemed to remark about the wind. Ash studied the sky a moment, then glanced back through the window.

Swift pulled Caius behind the window's curtain.

Ash and the three men set off across the car park.

When they were well across it and heading to the pier, Swift led Caius hustling out, to their car.

Tripping over each other, trying not to laugh out loud, they hauled from the trunk five packs holding their camping gear, each tucked inside waterproof plastic casings.

The cases were swollen with air, so bloated it was impossible to move them without rubbing them together, making them creak, which sounded exactly like Edric farting.

Swift could hardly breathe for laughing as Caius dragged him to the side of the tavern.

Keeping their load as quiet as possible, they peered around the corner.

Ash was crossing the beach now, following his sailors to the east end of the dock.

"That's lucky," whispered Caius. "Justus docks on the west end." He gestured for Swift to follow him.

Swift didn't move.

Caius waved him on. "The coast is clear."

Swift pointed. "You've got to be kidding me."

Ash and the three sailors turned down a long pier, beside which floated a vessel that dwarfed all the others.

This was no motorboat, like what Ash's father sailed. This was a full-masted brigantine.

The ship looked almost exactly like the *Regulus*. Except that it was bigger.

Caius shook his head. "We're dealing with an honest-to-God psycho."

Once Ash and the sailors had disappeared onto their ship, Swift and Caius ran for the west end of the dock. They raced down the pier stretching next to the *Regulus*.

Swift jumped into the ship and threw down his bubbles of waterproof cases, then took Caius' load. He dropped everything into the stow.

Caius stripped the ropes off their docking posts, then climbed aboard.

"The faster we can charge north," said Swift, "the better the chance we'll have of outrunning them."

But Caius was always reluctant to use the engine, wanting to save fuel in case they truly needed it.

Swift caught Caius' glance. "Can we use some fuel to make our escape?"

Caius climbed the steering platform. "You don't have to ask me twice."

Swift punched the air.

Caius gunned the engine. "Let's see if we can shake them. Loose the sails, and we'll fly."

Swift raced about the ship, unfastening her sails and setting each to catch the wind.

The *Strider*, tied at the stern, rallied with the *Regulus*, hopping wave after wave.

Swift glanced at the marina's east end.

Ash's monster brigantine had cleared the pack of docked ships and was angling their way.

"Bloody Helheim—he's seen us." Swift rushed to the steering deck and climbed up beside Caius. "What if he does try to follow? Can't you give it more juice?"

Caius killed the engine.

"Wait—what are you doing?"

"I'm not wasting fuel in a race that we're going to lose." He took the keys from the ignition and pocketed them.

"Aren't you feeling this wind, though?" Swift ducked to look beneath the sails toward the east.

Ash's brigantine was charging straight toward them.

"Help me fix the sails to better catch it," said Swift.

"Ash will catch this wind too." Caius climbed down from the steering deck. "And he could make more of it with all of those sails."

Swift followed Caius to the mainmast. "We can't just give up. We could still pull ahead."

"You're forgetting that Ash hired a crew." Caius slackened the mainsail and tied it off. "The two of us couldn't dream of working our sails fast enough to match that." He seemed to be calculating as he moved to the rail. "We're going to let them close in, because—a thought strikes me..."

Swift followed him. "For how to lose them?"

"It's a wild idea, but—how badly do you want to find the Star of Atlantis."

"What kind of question is that?" asked Swift. "You know I want to find it."

"Do you want it badly enough to welcome some real help?"

Swift narrowed his eyes. "What are you getting at?"

"Ash may have no idea where Sterncastle Cove is," said

Caius. "But he knows how to sail. And he's got a powerful ship with professional sailors."

There was no way Caius was suggesting that they team up with Ash.

Caius rested his gaze on Swift. "What if Ash came with us?"

Swift tripped back from him. "Did you not just call him a psycho?"

Caius held out his arm. "Listen—"

Swift jerked away. "If you think I'm working with that son of a cock up, then you're the one out of your mind."

"Hear me out. You with your research, he with his sailors—would we not have a winning chance of making the most of this chase?"

Swift couldn't look at Caius.

Focusing on anything, actually, was proving difficult, the way heat was spreading under his jacket, thickening in his chest, making even breathing a challenge.

Caius caught Swift's glance. "Think of it not as teaming with Ash, but teaming with those sailors he hired. We're about to go into some treacherous terrain. If we joined with them, we'd have some real help."

"I can't believe we're even talking about this."

"If we were to find the Star of Atlantis," said Caius, "I understand this would introduce the complexities of splitting it, but—would that not be worth it, to have a better shot altogether?"

"It's a terrible idea," said Swift. "There's no way Ash would go where we want. He'd just waste our time."

"I actually think he'd listen to you," said Caius. "If you were to invite him to join us, he'd have to show his cards. And my bet is that he'd cave. As arrogant as he is, even he'd have to admit that your theories are strong and worth following. After all, does he not want the same thing as you?"

Swift couldn't let Caius get a hold of this idea. When they argued, Caius almost always prevailed. If Caius decided Ash should come, he'd make it happen.

Swift struggled to conjure more points that would quickly get the notion out of Caius' head.

"What Ash wants is to crush me."

"Hang on," said Caius, "what if—"

Swift backed away from him. "This weekend was supposed to be about my dream, not his. It was meant to be about you and me doing something great together to celebrate my birthday, my last moment of freedom. Or have you forgotten that?"

"It is about us," said Caius. "And it's a celebration, for sure. But you'd be kidding yourself to say that it's only about us and not at all about finding the Star of Atlantis. If that's what you're after, then we'd have a far better shot with more hands on deck. That's all I'm suggesting."

Caius might say he had confidence in Swift. He might've come all this way to support Swift's dream.

But if he really believed in Swift, why was he suddenly thinking that they needed Ash, of all people—and professional sailors—to even have a shot?

The doubt Ash had cast over Swift seemed to be crystalizing on him, like a glazing of salt from a sea mist.

Swift threaded his hands into his hair. "I don't see how you could even imagine this."

He paced away.

Caius followed him. "It's just an idea. And maybe a good one."

"Just an idea." Swift faced him. "An idea that would force me to work with the person who hates me more than anything. An idea that would lose me any hope of laying my own hands on the Star of Atlantis."

"All right, all right," said Caius.

Swift couldn't stop his pacing.

"And finding the Star of Atlantis with Ash—the satisfaction would be a mere a fraction of how finding it on my own would feel."

"Calm down—"

"And maybe more hands would be helpful, ensuring safe

passage through wild water—but Ash isn't safe. He'd do nothing but complicate and sabotage and get in my head—"

"Hey." Caius caught Swift and held him in place. "Try to relax."

Swift worked to steady his voice. "I promise you. Any shot at camaraderie with Ash would fall flat. Ash takes advantage of gestures of friendship. It's how he operates."

Caius seemed to be noting the heat in Swift's face. He seemed regretful for causing it.

"I'll not say another word about it." Caius leaned back against the rail. "I suppose there's a small part of me that's hoped the two of you might mend things someday. I know how badly you've wanted that in the past. It just struck me that this might be a chance."

Caius who always hoped. Caius who never despaired. If only he were right.

"I've tried and tried," said Swift. "I thought you knew that."

Caius said nothing. He just squeezed Swift's shoulder. He knew.

Swift took a deep breath and let go of it.

Ash's ship—its sails broad and boastful—rolled close enough that her waves knocked the *Regulus*.

"Can I do the talking?" asked Swift.

Caius gave him a nod.

The leviathan brigantine pulled to a stop. Ash sauntered to its brassy rail.

"I thought I'd give you one last chance," Ash called. "If you want to have any hope of finding the Star of Atlantis, you'll have to follow me."

"We have our own strategy," Swift called above the wind.

"Suit yourself, but you can't say I didn't give you a fair shot." Ash pointed to the southern coast of Wales. "We're going to Swansea, along the southern side of the hook. Lots of coves there. Unexamined. Lots of promise."

"Best of luck," hollered Swift.

One of the sailors called out a question to Ash about the heading.

Ash gestured for the sailor to wait. "So, I told you my precise destination," he shouted down to Swift. "Will you not return the favor and tell me yours?"

"Far North Wales," called Swift, not missing a beat.

Caius glanced at him.

"Snowdonia. Up around Fairbourne."

Ash brightened some. "Searching the far north for a Welsh treasure thought to be stowed along the southern coasts...well, like you said—you have your own strategy."

"You done messing with us?" Swift shouted.

As irritated as he already was, from heat flashing into his face, from seeing Ash's smug contempt, from hearing his cruel dismissals and criticisms, Swift could hardly keep himself from screaming the words—"You can move off anytime."

"Cool it, Swift. All I was doing was trying to help." Ash nodded to his crew. "I was just trying to be a good sport."

"You're trying to ruin this," Swift shouted, "like you ruin everything."

Caius eased him down from the rail.

The engine on Ash's brigantine roared, and the ship with its glorious sails and its beefy crew pulled away.

Ash, from the stern, looked Swift straight in the eyes.

He saluted.

The sight of it struck Swift like he'd taken a blow to the chest.

That was what he himself had done just before Ash had tumbled over the dock into the water.

It was what Ash had read as a gesture meaning Swift wanted him to die.

That salute was Ash saying, "go to Hell."

And he meant it.

"Come on, lad." Caius, watching the ship grow smaller, watching Ash and his salute grow smaller, seemed to comprehend the gesture, too.

Swift held himself at the rail. Kept his gaze on the diminishing ship.

In watching Ash reflect that most painful moment—the

moment just before the both of them almost drowned—he saw a crystal-clear embodiment of all Ash's terrible accusations; of all the doubt and guilt and insecurity he'd cruelly cast at Swift over many years.

Cerebrally, he knew Ash was vicious, and he'd known it for some time. But at this moment, he felt Ash's treachery as keenly as if it'd been a knife driven into his heart. A knife that'd first pierced him on the day of the Tumble.

A knife that he found he could pull out if he wanted.

Finally, he understood what Edric had meant about refusing to take Ash's bait.

"I can see him," said Swift. "I finally can see him exactly as he is. There's truly not a bit of him that cares about me. He doesn't appreciate the Star of Atlantis, either. He really might not think that it's out there."

Caius watched Swift closely. "And what do you think?"

Swift met Caius' gaze. "I think I know where it is."

Caius gently smiled. "Take your eyes off that ship and don't look on it twice. You and I have business of our own."

Swift cleared wind-drawn tears from his eyes.

Caius threaded a coil of rope into Swift's hands. "Take the main."

11

Swift and Caius kept the *Regulus* flying all morning and into the late afternoon.

When the sun had crossed into the west and was warming the sea with tones of late afternoon gold, Swift finally tied off the mainsail and gave his hands a rest.

He watched Caius bustle to three other sails—watched him struggle to keep them in check.

The *Regulus* was still pacing well over the waves, and with every hour that'd passed, the vision of actually claiming the Star of Atlantis seemed more material.

But the weary look on Caius, the sight of the expanse of water unending, the icy chill washing in with the blue evening clouds—not to mention the tiredness marking Swift's own muscles—it altogether summoned a sense of vulnerability.

As wonderful as it felt to be out on the water, anticipating the moment when he might glimpse Sterncastle Cove, he couldn't shake down a persistent sense of being cornered with the wilds of the sea.

Caius, glancing at Swift, seemed to catch the hint of anxiety on him.

"The *Regulus* is a handful of ship for just two." He handed Swift a rope to coil. "But we're managing fine."

"Could we not use the engine?" asked Swift. "For a little ways at least."

"I was about to suggest the same thing. To be honest, I'm spent, and I bet you are, too. But we have to be careful not to waste fuel. It's better to work the sails all we can."

Swift winked up at Caius, standing tall on the center deck, backlit by the deepening blue sky. "Have you ever sailed the *Regulus* with just two before?"

"The summer you turned five, Justus and I took her out almost every weekend." Caius drew from the stow the windproof clothes they'd need as the temperature dropped with the sun. "That was just after he'd been given the *Regulus*, and he wanted to go all the time."

Swift received his windproof jacket and set of slacks from Caius. "How long will it take us, from here, to reach the first cove?"

Caius pulled out his phone and refreshed his calculation of the coordinates. "About two hours, I'd say, if we use the engine to sprint some. We should be nearing the coves before sunset."

At the mention of sunset, an image flashed in Swift's mind—himself slipping into the tall, angular doorway of a sea cavern; treading pebbles glazed with seawater, shining apricot and gold by the gently setting sun.

Caius following him in with a lantern; the two of them overjoyed with the sight of a treasure chest nestled in the back of the cave; the chest seeming luminous, all on its own, its sorrel wood and dark metal clasp shrouding its mystical treasure—the Star of Atlantis.

"So—before the sun even sets today," said Swift, "I might be laying my hands on the Star of Atlantis."

"Not quite so fast," said Caius. "Keep in mind, the sun might be setting when we reach the mouth of that first cove you wanted a look at. We'll have to anchor the *Regulus* there and put her to bed. It'll take some time, then, to work the *Strider* to the coast."

"We'll have to bring the treasure in on the *Strider* by loads!"

Swift worked his trainers through the legs of the waterproof trousers.

"Think we're going to have a big haul, do you?" Caius knelt and helped Swift maneuver the soles of his shoes through the cuffs.

Sealed in the night-sailing waterproof suit, Swift grew almost immediately hot, despite the chill in the wind, despite that the sun angling westward was falling behind clouds.

"As legendary as the Star of Atlantis is," said Swift, "I bet it's more marvelous than even I could imagine." He unzipped the front of his suit.

Caius zipped Swift's suit back tight. "What do you think it'll be?" He settled into the captain's chair and adjusted the wheel to their course.

"Picture this."

Swift hung onto the steering deck as the boat quickened.

"We reach the cove, and inside we find the ring of rocks. They'll be blackened and salt-stained like Kraken teeth would be—exactly the way my book describes. The rocks will surround a high islet, just like a sterncastle on a ship. The rocks would keep the waves mostly out, so the cavern, where the treasure rests, would never flood."

"You've given this quite a bit of thought," said Caius.

Swift couldn't really see Caius anymore. He could only see his vision of Sterncastle Cove.

"Inside the cavern waits a magnificent chest," said Swift. "It's shining like it might really hold a blazing star. And when we open it, piles of galleons spill out—the wealth plundered by Cynfael Maddox to give to the poor. On top of the money, there's a layer of rubies, sapphires, diamonds, and pearls. Next up are the tyrant king's personal artifacts—taken just for spite: plates and goblets and platters, swords and scythes, arrows, spears, and armor. Everything would be forged of precious metals.

"And on the very top of the stash stands a shining, golden chest—a chest with a silver Celtic star inlaid—like what's drawn on my map and my book. The chest is studded with diamonds. And inside the chest: there rests the Star of Atlantis."

"And what, do you imagine, is the Star of Atlantis?" asked Caius.

Though Swift could see everything else as clear as crystal, when he tried to picture the Star of Atlantis itself, he could see nothing.

The sight of Caius and the silvering ocean clarified.

"No idea." Swift clenched his fists, shaking the imagined sensation of sharp gemstones and cold metal on his palms.

"You've probably read all that's been written about the Star of Atlantis." Caius glanced at the swell of a heightening wind fluttering the sails. "Does no one speculate about what it might be?"

"There is speculation, but it's known to be just speculation. I've read over and over that the Star of Atlantis is something precious to sailors. I've no doubt that it's extraordinary. If it were something common, I think it'd either be clearly remembered, or forgotten entirely."

Caius glanced beyond Swift at the sails, then killed the engine. "The wind's really picking up. We should take advantage of that. We'll conserve quite a lot of fuel by catching this gale and letting it carry us a while. We won't move as quick, but it'd be prudent." He climbed down from the steering deck. "I'm up for another run with the sails, now. Are you?"

"No, let's move quick," said Swift. "It seems we'd want to reach Sterncastle Cove while we still have as much daylight as possible."

"It won't matter." Caius loosened the top rope to widen the mainsail. "Even if we flew to it with full power, we wouldn't have time to scout much of anything before dark."

"But, sailing through Sterncastle Cove to the shore in the *Strider*, we'll have to glide right past the islet. We could just hop onto it for a minute."

"Hop onto it?" Caius handed Swift a rope. "When the sun's setting and the temperature's plummeting? When we haven't studied the terrain of the islet, nor the waves, nor a method for making it into or out of the cove? When we haven't yet set up our base camp on the beach? No chance of talking me into that."

The tone in Caius' voice was pitched with a panic Swift didn't hear often in him.

Could he be affected, too, by this wide rocking water and the imminent night?

But Caius was always so positive and confident. Surely, he wasn't afraid.

Swift wound his treasure-itchy hands tightly inside the rope. "We must have fuel enough for a little more sprinting." He watched Caius to see if the tinge of anxiety might leave him.

"I'll tell you what," said Caius. "Let's work the sails for a while. Once we get close to the cove, we can use the engine to make our final run. That way you'll get to watch our approach to the cove, rather than having to focus on the sails."

Swift studied the open sky with its eastern edge deepening, and the sun in its western hemisphere swelling with evening.

The idea of night falling on these deep waters agitated the restlessness he'd been suffering all afternoon, watching Caius at the sails struggling against the blustery wind. And the ache in his own body, keener now at the end of the day, heightened his sense of exposure to the sea and its strength.

Getting into the cove and safely to shore as quickly as possible, when they still had some light and a little more warmth, seemed a much safer plan.

"Wouldn't we need some daylight, though, to make it to the coast?" asked Swift. "Sprinting on would do nothing but help us reach the shore safely. Did we not load in a surplus of fuel?"

Caius shook Swift off the rope he was tightening and corrected his grip. "It's never wise to spend your reserves to reach your destination." He pushed in front of Swift and fixed the ropes yet tighter. "That's how sailors get marooned. They conserve nothing for the journey home."

Swift traced the tower of the mast and its full sails, straining north.

"We might have a good enough wind to drive us back to Devon without any fuel."

Caius cast Swift a cautioning look.

Swift went to the ship's rail. "We wouldn't be in a hurry on the way home. We'd have our treasure."

The patience that usually softened Caius' expression was waning. "If we tuck these sails in too early, we might find ourselves without fuel or wind."

Swift peered down at the water, at the strong northern waves breaking on the hull. "Why is it not better to use more fuel now, when night's coming and when the temperature's dropping, and when the water might roughen, and when who knows what might rise from the deeps."

Caius joined Swift at the rail. He stared at the great dark waves rocking the boat, jarring the *Regulus* and the *Strider* alike, as though he, too, were wondering what night would bring.

"Are you feeling a bit nervous about taking on a rough cove in the *Strider*?" asked Caius.

"No." Swift tried to soften his voice. "It just feels like we need to hurry now. We could make it home as slowly as we pleased."

"Let's try not to let our impatience to get to your cove compromise our better judgement." Caius opened another sail.

"I'm not being impatient," said Swift. "It's just—"

But Caius, hurrying across the bow, busying himself with unleashing sails, was finished listening.

Swift shook his hands, working out the stiffness and tension from dealing with the canvas and ropes.

They hungered, it was true, to touch the islet in the middle of the cove—an islet he'd waited practically his whole life to reach. He was anxious, of course, to learn whether his leads would pay off.

But it wasn't impatience making him argue so resolutely with Caius. It absolutely was fear. And the hardening on Caius' face betrayed that fear was indeed taking hold of him too.

Caius, his brow raised, glanced at Swift.

He was waiting for cooperation.

Swift put his aching hands to work on the center deck. He cloaked the threatening sense of night falling in the tough work of handling sails.

12

*S*ailing wasn't so much an act of muscle, as it was an act of will.

The will to sail usually outlasted the body—kept the tired body going despite the lilt of the deck and the blasts of tempestuous wind.

The wind had been steady though, carrying the *Regulus* as quickly as she was capable of sailing, hurrying Swift and Caius to what might lie along the untamed shores of north Pembrokeshire.

Way out in the sea, Swift occasionally spotted the sails of rare fishing boats cutting the sky. But the coasts remained barren and wild, the Wentletrap Forest at times almost touching the water, and in some places drawn back like a blackish green serpent, asleep in a stillness of mist.

The *Regulus* plowed on, moving beyond the craggy shore to stretches of pale beaches gently arcing around blue topaz waters, smooth as glass.

Swift hung in as the late day wore on, kept an eye on the movement of the coast.

He watched each emerging horizon, noticing the shifting topographies and comparing the coastal landscape to the block print of Sterncastle Cove.

The sun finally sank like a stone toward the sea, and in concord with its dimming, the wind weakened.

The coastal edge shifted from wilder waters framed by seashell white beaches to a series of handsome crags.

The *Regulus* had to be closing in on the waters of the coordinates he'd targeted.

After working the ship for this long, Swift's back and legs were stiffening, and his fingers were iced and barely would bend.

The wetsuit and windbreaker were keeping his core warm enough—too warm, actually.

Bit by bit, he'd managed to unzip it halfway without Caius intervening.

Caius looked just as tired as Swift felt, just as frigid and sore —but he also seemed just as determined.

In bursts when the wind pulled the ship strongly, when it seemed they were making fast headway, the notion rose to suggest to Caius again that perhaps they'd have time for some exploring tonight.

But as quickly as those gales visited, they'd vanish, leaving the *Regulus* just inching over the darkening sea.

If one of the two coves he'd chosen did reveal itself plainly as Sterncastle Cove, Swift knew himself well enough to anticipate that the impulse to investigate it would strengthen even more.

But he had to keep their safety as the highest priority. Unless Caius changed his mind and suggested exploring, Swift resolved not to press any urgency he might feel to go searching tonight.

When the sun at last touched its shine to the water, Caius caught Swift's gaze and held it.

A fresh brightness on him told Swift that they were indeed closing in on the coordinates of the first cove.

"We'll have to scout your cove by eye from here." Caius showed Swift his phone. "The signal sputtered along a bit further than I expected, but now we've definitely lost it."

Swift took the phone. "How will we track the coordinates without your phone?"

Caius pulled out their notes. "We're within three miles of where the nearest set of coordinates pointed." He knelt before a storage trunk and unboxed a spyglass.

Swift took the spyglass and aimed it at the coast.

The waterline here sprawled with rock crags hacked up by the sea. The inland shore transformed to weeds and waving shore grasses standing before the dark ramparts of the Wentletrap Forest.

Swift trained the spyglass on the water.

His first impulse was to look for the blue shimmering he'd seen before, when he stole away with the *Strider* and sailed to what he thought might be Sterncastle Cove.

The water showed nothing but blackness and murk—just dinginess tinted by a crystalish green cast of chill that seemed to strike to the bone, making Swift zip his jacket to his chin.

A second glance through the spyglass landed him a glimpse of a curious seal, but nothing of the fantastical sort that the *Star of Atlantis* book and map prescribed would be skulking around Sterncastle Cove.

Not that he really expected to see a mermaid or the Kraken. But he very well might see something wondrous that he couldn't explain.

Nothing else presented itself, though, besides seaweed.

Swift trained the spyglass on the distant land to the north.

With the dimming of the sky, it was growing difficult to make out the fine details of the coast.

"Is there no chance of getting the signal back?" asked Swift. "I'm afraid that I might miss our cove."

"The Wentletrap Forest is a preserve," said Caius. "It's wholly undeveloped. Wild. There won't be any more cell towers between here and Cardiganshire." He handed Swift a thick stocking cap and a pair of gloves.

Swift put them on, then peered again through the spyglass toward the waterline on the horizon.

"If we think we're getting close to Sterncastle Cove," said

Swift, "maybe we should survey the shallows for mermaids. If we spotted one, she might guide us straight to where the Star of Atlantis is hidden."

Caius raised his brow. "Tell me you're joking. You are joking, right?"

Swift shrugged. "You never know."

Caius pointed at another seal in the water. "There's your mermaid."

The seal stared at them with liquidy eyes as they passed.

"I don't know if anyone reports seeing mermaids anymore," said Caius. "But in older days, when people were more prone to believe in the fantastical, what sailors thought to be mermaids often turned out to be dolphins or seals."

"I'll give you that," said Swift. "But how many reports come in about sea creatures that can't be identified?"

"How treacherous…" said Caius.

"Sure, some reports are fearsome," said Swift. "Still—"

But Caius wasn't looking at Swift anymore. He was watching the shoreline.

The land was rising into cliffs that stretched into the sea, the water around them tending rough.

Staring at the patches of white water twisting around the cliffs, Caius drifted across the ship and stood closely beside Swift at the rail.

"Those coastal draws are breaking hard," said Caius. "It's possible that we'll find the entrance to any coves around here a bit fussy."

"Sterncastle Cove would be fussy, if it's anything like the woodblock print," said Swift. "If gulls are wheeling over it, we might find its white waters swarming with mermaids and their kills."

Caius glanced at him. "You do realize that you're going to be fourteen tomorrow."

Swift lowered his gaze to the water, upheaved by the *Regulus* and racing away.

It seemed, in a deep place in the core of his chest, that the possibility of sighting mermaids, or his book's other creatures, wasn't just a fantasy.

There were plenty of sailors, even nowadays, who claimed to have seen mythical things.

The thought brought some comfort. Not all mermaids were thought to be murderous. For every horror tale of mermaids drowning an unwary sailor, there was another of mermaids rescuing shipwreck victims.

"If Sterncastle Cove is bound to be treacherous," said Swift, "it seems more worth battling if there are supernatural forces, like mermaids, at play."

"What would Justus say if he heard you going on about mermaids like that?" asked Caius. "What would Edric say?"

Swift leaned on the rail and focused more concertedly on the water. "Justus would tell me to focus on the animals and plants I might actually chance to see—although he wouldn't dismiss the possibility of running across something mysterious. Edric would flat out tell me to grow up."

"So do you think maybe you shouldn't let yourself carry on like this?"

"Come on," said Swift. "Don't you think entertaining the lore of sea legends is part of the fun of sailing?"

"The thing is," said Caius, "you are growing up. If Justus has his way, he'll have you grown up by the time you take those exams. Because of that, I fear a bit for you."

Swift shrugged. "I know I'm growing up."

"So, can you picture a fourteen-year-old lad, a lad aiming to test his way into a medical Practicum, giving as much thought as you do to pirates and mermaids? Or could you picture any fourteen-year-old talking like you are, for that matter?"

Even while some parts inside him felt more aligned with Caius and Justus, the part of Swift that loved all this venturing and legend conjuring was certainly alive and well. And here, on the wild Celtic Sea, it felt necessary to hang on to that part of himself.

Besides, despite all the pale seriousness marring Caius,

Swift couldn't buy that he wasn't just a little excited about the possibility that more exists than what's explainable.

"You yourself have a great imagination," said Swift. "Who are you to cast shame at me for giving a few fantasies a bit of room to breathe?"

Caius closed in. "Between you and me, do you think you're truly ready to start in on those studies?"

That brought Swift to staring up at Caius.

Earlier, Caius had cast doubts about whether Swift could find the Star of Atlantis—which, though a little maddening, was at least understandable.

Was he now casting doubt about Swift's competence to take on the entrance trials and exams?

"What kind of question is that?" asked Swift. "You yourself said you believe that I'm capable."

"Don't get me wrong, I know you're skilled enough. It's just —you'd have to love medicine the way you love legends in order to score high enough—(read, perfect)—on the Practicum exams and its trials. Do you think that you love it like that?"

Swift had never thought about medicine, or studying, in terms of love. The closest he could come to feeling a love for medicine—the only real heart's pull he felt toward the medical Practicum—was the admiration he felt for Caius.

"From where I stand, how would I even know if I loved it?" asked Swift.

"I knew." Caius leaned on the rail. "Even though I was just a couple of years older than what you are now—I knew medicine was where I belonged."

"So, if I don't know right this minute that I'd love it, you think I'm doomed to fail?"

"No, but I'd like you to realize how wholly you'll have to dedicate yourself to prep for that competition."

It felt odd that Caius seemed suddenly so worried about Swift's Practicum trials and exams, when an immediate challenge of difficult waters and rough sailing was approaching.

Swift took a step back. "Why are you bringing this up now?"

"I need to know whether you realize what it'll be like, spending all your days and most of your nights reading medical texts. And if you get accepted, it'll be four long years of tough work. Can you conceptualize that?"

Swift knew all this, of course.

"Why are you ignoring my question?" asked Swift. "Why are you wanting to talk about this now?"

Now, when the sunset was tending red, and when there was a cove with exciting, possibly enchanted waters to reach, and a treasure to find—a treasure known to be mythical and yet likely real—which Swift might very well have figured out how to scout? Why talk about the Practicum now, when the water flashing white against the coastal rocks seemed to be growing rougher? The wind colder?

"Your next few years will be spent going at the Practicum full-time." Caius pulled Swift's hat tighter over his head. "And when classes are in session, it'll be like trying to get all your work done while having the hardest part-time job imaginable."

"Do you think I haven't considered how difficult it's going to be?" The question came more strongly than Swift meant it to.

But it felt so artificial for Caius to be stressing out about Swift's Practicum now.

It seemed like Caius was attempting to cloak the fear Swift was reading on him.

Or worse—was he trying to sneak some sort of agenda into this trip?

Caius eyed him sidelong. "You'll have no choice but to set aside monsters and mermaids and pirates and treasures and fame. None of that belongs where you're headed."

"This sea venturing," said Swift. "This country of blues shifting to silvers. This waving world of open sunsets and wide sweeps of water and nothing to stifle the ascension of stars...this is, without question, a place I belong."

And it was a place Swift would soon lose.

"But that doesn't mean that I don't also feel drawn to medicine," said Swift.

"Do me a favor," said Caius. "Give the Practicum some hard

thinking over the weekend, all right? Justus is far out of touch, and it's just you and me out here in these elements that you love —this blue water and bright sunset and the stars soon to appear. Take advantage of that. I'd be glad to talk over medicine, and the Practicum, and your dreams, and your plans, as much as you'd like."

With all these cautioning words mingling in the wind, a bit of the joy in this venture seemed to have evaporated.

"And what if I don't want to talk about it?" asked Swift. "What if I want a break from thinking about it at all?"

"You'd be doing yourself a great favor to be honest with yourself," said Caius, "and with me. Because..."

Caius gazed again across the water, toward a line of roaring white eddies battering a cliffside.

"I feel I just need to caution you," said Caius. "Don't start in with Justus unless you're absolutely sure it's where you want to be."

Caius had the tendency to go all business like this when he sensed some intensity, some risk.

Maybe that's what all this was about. Maybe he was just dealing with some stress from thinking about taking on these rough waters.

This serious side of him was probably a trait that would pay off in medicine. But it tended to blow the fun out of things.

"If you think Justus would have it," said Swift, "if I told him that I wanted out—you're insane."

"Justus has pushed you, it's true," said Caius. "Has he pressured you too much? He's made it clear that the decision is yours."

Truly, Swift felt some honest confidence about the Practicum.

But hearing Caius' words of caution, feeling his doubts, looking at tall Caius—Caius, so assured of who he was and where he belonged—Caius with his gently-strong-soon-to-be-doctor's hands gripping the rail, his head now higher than the weakening sun...it made Swift's stomach drop.

Standing beside Caius was like standing at the foot of a mountain. Atmospheres divided him from Caius.

"So let it be your decision," said Caius. "Not mine, or Justus', or Edric's, or anyone's. Yours."

Swift spent a moment adjusting his gloves.

Their venture seemed, now, somewhat of a ploy.

A device to push him into confronting the difficulty of what lay ahead. A contrivance to coax Swift to let go of childish things.

Or—what if Caius was using this trip as a means to force Swift to recognize some devastating lack? A lack that perhaps Caius saw in him but couldn't bring himself to speak of forthright.

Swift folded his arms, hid his hands, so Caius wouldn't see how small, how weak they seemed, compared to his own.

Caius shifted toward him. "Look, I get that it's fun to pretend about sea legends. And I do hope that we find your treasure. But why not set the fantasies aside and instead focus on the true task at hand?"

"Is the task at hand not sea legends?" asked Swift. "Is the task at hand not winning the Star of Atlantis?"

"Even if you find the Star of Atlantis—" Caius looked down. Away.

Anxiety this intense on Caius was rare. And the degree of urgency slipping into his face was alarming.

Caius again met Swift's gaze. "A moment of victory, of finding a treasure, won't carry you at all in the Practicum. The Star of Atlantis is no shortcut to becoming who you are. I just need to know that you get that."

It was as though Caius was, with some desperation, trying to help Swift understand a point that he feared they might never talk over again.

Swift nodded, his face prickling with the heat from the tension he was sensing on Caius. "I get it."

A closer stretch of white waters, a stone's throw from them now, drew Caius' gaze.

As formidable, as threatening as those waters looked, they brought some relief.

Caius was focusing on them now, rather than on Swift—breaking a bit beneath the severity of his words.

Caius turned away and set to closing down the sails, his expression far removed from his ordinary humor.

He looked pale. Flat out troubled.

Swift toyed with the spyglass, glancing through it at the thrashing water ahead.

But he kept his eyes mostly on Caius—handling the lines in a rough way, his sternness snapping sails closed like he was clipping bird wings—silencing bird wings.

Caius glanced at Swift. "Help me by putting the mizzen to bed. We'll coast on the engine until you key in on where you'd like to stop. Then we can load up the *Strider* and ride her into your cove."

Caius seemed to be trying to brighten his expression, seemed to be wanting to sound fun-loving again—like he knew he'd drained out some of their fun and was regretful.

Swift helped him batten down the mizzen, the jib, then he settled against the bow with his father's spyglass.

13

The temper of the sea underneath the *Regulus* looked frolicky, every wave a small cheer from the Atlantic to brighten hunters chasing lost treasure, every gull's shrill cry rallying their onward advance through the sunset-streaked autumn waters.

Swift let the gulls' joy blow into him until Caius' cautioning tumbled well to the back of his mind, where it seemed to lose its power over him.

Caius climbed into the steering deck and charged the engine.

The *Regulus* slipped through calm waves as the sun's dying ember turned dark red and cast a bloody grin on the water.

Swift kept his spyglass trained on the scalloped coast and searched for the telltale signs of Sterncastle Cove.

After a few minutes, a bulb of jetting land—a long sandbar—emerged.

Caius revved the ship and rounded it.

The interior stretch of the sandbar sloped into soft ripples of hills that faded into the silt of a white beach, arrow straight, as far as Swift could see.

Five more minutes of sailing along the shore brought a patch of dark rocks to prominence.

Swift climbed onto the rail and scoped them.

Just beyond those rocky outcrops, the sea cut a deep gash into the coast—the arc of a magnificent cove.

Its white turbulence was as rough as any of the coastal waters they'd seen. Maybe rougher. At the mouth of the cove, a dense mist was gathering.

And inside the cove...a flutter of crimson, sunset-splashed wings.

Flocks of circling shore birds.

"It's Sterncastle Cove." Swift lowered the scope.

A tingling in his belly and the kick of his heart seemed to confirm it.

"It's Sterncastle Cove," he called to Caius.

Caius quickened the ship.

A few minutes of clipping parallel to shore, and the *Regulus* arrived, nose to nose, with the ragged rocks lining the cove's southern edge.

Caius steered the *Regulus* alongside the rocks, keeping skillfully clear of their sloshing. He steadied her at the cove's mouth and held her idling.

The *Regulus* rocked at the foot of two towering boulders—squared and oddly same-heighted—so much like two giant molars.

Swift, staring up at them, backed toward Caius. "Kraken teeth."

The great rocks looked like barbicans on a palace, twisting, cobbled of gnarly dark stones. Between them, where a castle portcullis could've been, spread a misty stretch of sea.

If these Celtic waters did hold monsters, this threshold seemed the onset of their welcome.

High above and inside the cove whirled the white-and-gray cyclone of carrion birds—gulls and petrels and ravens—some diving and others just riding the column of misty air.

And Swift, peering through that mist toward the dead center of the cove, spied an islet of towering rocks.

From here, the islet looked to be a rough cluster. But

drawing near it in the *Strider* might very well show it shaped like a ring as round as Earth.

Now that they were here, the sense of dread seemed to lighten from Swift's heart. The water looked rough, yes, but he and Caius could handle anything.

And the reward for their boldness might be the Star of Atlantis.

"When the shore draws long and straight," Swift whispered, *"skim the briny banks. Be swallowed by Sterncastle Cove. Seek the islet, round as Earth, studded with Kraken fangs. Mind the deeps for mermaid tails, shimmering blue and green. Heed their song, but touch the water not, lest your life be forfeit to their goddess. Always keep a weather eye on the mist coiling in the cove, for through it paddles old Grog Blossom, always dead, yet ever awake, cursed to forever sail as watchman over the Star of Atlantis."*

Caius stilled the engine. He went to their store of supplies.

Swift dropped the anchor and hurried to tow the *Strider* to the starboard flank. He climbed over the rail and dropped into the teetering dinghy.

Caius appeared at the rail and tossed down the bubbled gear packs.

They operated in unison, their procedure smooth, as though they'd drilled the exercise of transferring vacuum-sealed packs of camping gear from the *Regulus* to the *Strider* a thousand times.

Swift studied the hundred-meter stretch of white water between the mouth of the cove and the beach. "How long do you think it'll take us to reach the shore?" he called. "Will we manage it before dark?"

"If we hurry and make the most of the wind, we'll have no problem." Caius climbed down the ropes and landed beside Swift in the *Strider*. "There'll be no getting out of the dinghy on that islet tonight, though. Are we clear on that? Those rocks will be slick, and it'd be foolish to test them at twilight."

Swift studied the islet.

From even this stretching distance, he could make out how

jagged its boulders were, how sharp its pinnacles, piercing the sea mist. How treacherous.

And a smell of death lingered in the wind.

Something died in this cove that had to have perished days ago. Whatever killed it was probably hunting again.

"We'll build a snug base camp and tuck in early," said Caius. "Doesn't that sound good? Then we'll get up early and explore the islet at dawn. The tide will be nice and low, then, and will give us more footholds."

Swift made a place for Caius beside him on the *Strider's* bench. He handed Caius an oar.

14

Swift and Caius swept the sea together, angling the *Strider* into white waters.

Could this really be Sterncastle Cove?

Sterncastle Cove, where Cynfael Maddox hid the treasure of sailors and kings.

If it was, Sterncastle Cove was a mist world. A shadow world.

Vapor hung over the sea in a white way that seemed thicker than regular coastal mist.

There was something unhealthy about it, like volcanic fumes—like what Swift imagined would rise from the eleven rivers converging in the Nordic dark of pre-creation.

Sailing through the columns of ragged rocks studding the entrance to the cove, Swift and Caius found no track of water steady, and they had to fight to keep their bearing toward the more open channels, clear of jetting reefs.

Those reefs projecting from the skim looked like spear-tips frozen in stone, razor sharp and mineral-burned from a hundred million scuffles with the sea.

"Whoa, look out—" Caius struck out his oar to push back from a reef.

Swift threw his weight into the balance, helped meter the *Strider* until they cleared the reef and were rocking wide away.

"Can we manage this?" Swift alternated between paddling and gripping the edge of the *Strider* as waves tipped up her nose. "Should we turn back?"

"Turning isn't possible. We're all right, but help me aim to make straight for the beach. We have to keep clear of the reefs, of the eddies."

The islet in the core of the cove sure enough looked shaped like an almost-perfect circle. And its outermost boulders, sprawling about ten feet inward, seemed broad and flat enough to stand on.

The steep inner tower—twenty feet high or so—looked rough enough to support a climb, for glimpsing to see if a cave yawned within.

Fishing birds still swirled overhead, though their squabble had diminished with the going of the sun, some wanderers peeling off to roost on the desolate shore.

The further Swift and Caius advanced toward the beach, the stench of whatever the birds were feasting on sharpened.

It was the worst smell Swift had ever faced. It was acrid like a sack of garbage, sharp—like rain on rust. It coaxed visions of liquefying flesh, of eyes torn from a bloated cadaver.

"What is that?" called Swift, above the crashing of waves. "Can you see a carcass?"

"Water's too rough," said Caius. "We'll be able to see it from shore."

A wave raced up on Swift's side and soaked him.

He gasped and dropped his oar in his lap.

"Hang in." Caius lifted the oar back into Swift's hands.

Swift didn't take it. Couldn't take it. Frigid water had drenched his suit and sloshed in through the neck.

"We'll be through the worst of this once we're beyond the islet," said Caius. "The water on the far side looks quieter."

Swift sat frozen. Dripping. Breathless.

"Swift, I need you to paddle. It'll take both of us to get through this rough patch."

Swift mastered his muscles well enough to grip the oar and strike it into the sea.

After a moment, the motion generated some heat, and he could draw deeper breaths.

He spotted a line of easier water winding toward the islet, and then off again to the center of the cove. From there, it seemed to pull straight to the beach.

"Let's follow that," Swift managed to shout. "That draw looks calmer."

"I see it." Caius plunged his oar into a wave and aimed the *Strider* toward the bend in the water.

Her hull leapt, then charged into the heave of a current.

Its pull was so strong that they had to fight to keep the *Strider* from angling sideways.

"If we flip," said Caius, "say what we'd do."

The icy water still had some grip on Swift, making breathing still difficult. "Let's not flip."

"Talk to me," called Caius. "Tell me what we'd do."

Swift guarded his face against a splash. "I'm to hang on to whatever I can."

"That's right." Caius held his oar in the water to master the *Strider's* rocking. "And what will I do?"

"You're going to go under the water, but you'll be all right. You'll get your bearings, then you'll find me and right the *Strider*."

"Who's going to climb aboard first?"

"I am," said Swift. "I'm to stabilize the *Strider* while you climb in."

"Okay." Caius braced his feet against the planks. "We're closing in on the islet. I'll guide the *Strider* to break right and catch that current forking to the coast. Sit tight. Get ready to beat the sea."

Swift held his oar in the air. Caius speared the water and turned the craft sharp toward the coast.

Swift locked his legs against the bench and readied himself for the fight.

A wave kicked back from the islet and jolted the *Strider*

high. She crashed down, her starboard flank striking the tip of a reef.

Caius threw his weight to center the craft, but waves pummeled her down and spilled her onto her side.

Swift snatched for the *Strider's* sail, for her ropes, but waves snapped her away and sucked him into the sea.

Encased in ice water.

No variance anyplace.

No difference between down and up.

No air.

Swift spun until he was too dizzy to think. He let bubbles out while the sea tossed him, his hands outstretched and clawing.

His fingers brushed something hard and sharp. He gripped with both hands and pulled.

He opened his eyes and found himself out of the waves, sea water leeching from his mouth.

Caius had him by the back of the jacket and was hauling him onto the islet's rock shelf.

Swift tried to do his part to scramble up it, but his limbs were frozen. Caius dragged Swift's legs fully onto the shelf.

Caius held him tight. "Speak if you're breathing."

"I'm numb."

"Keep hold here," Caius trained Swift's hands to a crevice in the shelf.

Swift worked his knees beneath him.

"I'm going to try to right the *Strider*," said Caius.

Swift gripped the rock shelf with one hand, and with the other snagged Caius' jacket.

Caius tried to unhook Swift's hand from it, but Swift refused to let go.

Caius moved as far out as Swift would let him. He dragged the *Strider* closer by her tow rope. He tried to manipulate her off her side, but it was no use.

She was waterlogged, full tilt, the suck of an eddy the only force keeping her within reach. It looked like her starboard hull was punctured.

Caius could just touch the handle of the *Strider*'s stow, and he opened it.

Their vacuum-packed bags floated out.

"Get ready to receive cargo," called Caius.

Swift dragged himself into a crouch.

With dead-fingered hands, with iced arms moving like mechanical clubs, he took piece after piece from Caius—plastic packs holding clothes, bedrolls, their cooler, camping gear, Caius' medical bag.

The rock supporting Swift spread inward just deeply enough that he could stack the bundles. The islet's shelf trailed around its center tower like a pathway, about twenty feet back until it curved out of sight.

When the unloading was done, the sun was fully gone. All that remained in the west was a dim crimson splash—the vanished day star coiling its colors out of the waves.

Swift shimmied away from the shelf's edge and tipped onto his side against the crook of the rock tower.

He couldn't wholly fathom what'd just happened; couldn't believe the *Strider* was wrecked; couldn't grasp how he and Caius were still alive.

And what would Ash think when he heard what became of Swift's chase.

If he knew how close to drowning Swift had just come, would Ash feel they were even now, Swift's role in Ash's near-death rectified?

Or would Ash just start composing his own plans to chase the treasure Swift had failed to claim?

Swift steadied his breathing as he watched Caius tighten the *Strider*'s stow.

The tower behind him was high enough to block some of the wind, but the spray coming off the biggest waves reached him, making him shiver still harder.

Caius crowded their packs further away from the edge, then crawled to Swift. He felt Swift's cheeks and fingers, laid his hand against Swift's chest, then unzipped Swift's windbreaker and pulled it off him.

Swift lay shivering on the bare rock as Caius worked as much water out of Swift's wetsuit as he could.

The suit wasn't warm, but it was keeping the bite of the chilled air at bay.

Caius clapped his hands every minute or so to keep blood in them, but it seemed he was having difficulty bending his fingers.

Swift tried to sit up, to reach to hold Caius' hands, but his muscles wouldn't respond. He tried to speak, but his lips felt swollen.

"Do you hurt anyplace?" asked Caius.

Swift shook his head.

Caius struggled to unzip his own windbreaker. When he managed it, he peeled it off and pressed down his own wetsuit. He wedged their two jackets high on the islet's tower where they could dry in the wind.

He dragged near one of the plastic packs and hauled out two hooded wool pullovers. He stretched one on, then worked Swift's arms and head into the other.

He fished out a couple of heat packs from his medical kit. He tucked one inside his own pullover pocket, then wrapped Swift's hands around the other.

The heat pack was a handful of heaven. Swift gripped it until he could move his fingers, then he snugged it into the neckline of his suit.

The heat bathing his frozen face felt like blades, but in a few minutes, the frostbite weakened, leaving him in a sleepy lukewarmth.

Caius eased Swift back beside him against the rock tower, unfolded a blanket, and wrapped them both.

"Can we stay on this ledge all night?" Swift asked. "Will the water rise?"

"We're coming off high tide. This rock shelf should stay above the waves for some time."

It wasn't much comfort. Swift was still shivering, thawing just by increments.

And with the blackening water, its violence, its roar—with

night's descent sapping the sky and sea of all color—a sense swelled of predators leering beneath the sharp waves.

If any Kraken really haunted this place, it might be coming.

And even if the Kraken remained locked in legends, without a doubt—here swam sharks.

15

The sand on the distant shore shone silvered. The dryness of its beach, the cover of its trees looked like salvation.

Backlit by the rising moon, the waterline seemed to glow, like it was radiating warm light.

But even if that beach seemed like a refuge, it might not be. Its beauty might just be a trick of the twilight. Reaching it, they might find nothing but colder wind and a thicker mist.

Or they might discover the coast to be the Norse fire world —a place seamed to the mist world with currents of toxic water; a place so treacherous that even gods couldn't survive, burning sand swallowing them the instant they set foot on shore.

Swift shook his head clear of the vision of Norse Hell and instead pictured a reasonable, plain, dry beach. With a fire going on it. Where the rotten-carcass smell wouldn't be so pungent.

Tears stung his eyes from wanting it so badly.

"Maybe together we could free the *Strider*," Swift said, over the ruckus of whooshing waves. "Sail her to shore."

"No point in wasting our effort," said Caius. "She's logged. We'll have to call the coast guard to tow her out."

Caius untangled himself from the blanket and wrapped it

all around Swift. He caught the dinghy's line and did his best to fix it firmer to a rocky knob.

The knot Caius tied was good, but Swift had practiced a better one.

He slid out his heat pack and gripped it a moment. "I know a firmer hold." He scooted to the edge.

Caius held on to a loop on Swift's suit as Swift stood and loosed the knot.

His fingers, no longer numb, but stiff—a sensation he'd grown accustomed to in sailing—cooperated, and in a moment the knot was undone.

He spied a higher, sturdier-looking knob. He wove the strands into the loose form of his knot. He widened its loop and cast the rope over the projection, two meters up. The knot tightened when the *Strider* pulled away.

The line kept her wedged well. Her scraping against the rocks quieted.

Caius studied the taut line. "Well done." He crowded Swift back to the tower wall.

Swift eased closely against Caius, opening the blanket. "What are we going to do?"

"You tell me," said Caius. "What are our most basic survival goals?"

"Warmth. Freshwater."

"Right. So, we'll eat and drink some, then calculate our options for getting someplace our clothes can stay dry. Someplace we can make a fire."

Swift eyed the crown of the islet's tower, stretching twenty feet up toward the stars.

It was broad enough that there really might be a sea cavern inside. A place protected from wind. Maybe in there, it would even be dry.

Swift carefully stood. "I could climb this rock face and look over its edge. The inside might be protected from the wind."

Caius stood, too, guarding Swift from sea spray. "These rocks are impassible." He touched them. "Slick with algae."

Swift peered into a split between two rocks. "Let's at least shine a light in there. What if there's a cave? What if it's dry inside?"

Caius fished a torch from one of the bags. He shone it through the split rock.

Swift peered beneath him, into the crack.

The light struck the white belly of a crab.

It tiptoed away, unveiling the interior space like a curtain drawn.

The chamber inside the tower stole what little breath Swift had. There was no glut of treasure sleeping in a sparkling pile, but other than that, this was so alike to his fantasy of how a cavern holding the Star of Atlantis might look.

Crabs were plentiful, tapping their arrow-tipped feet along the moist rocks. It seemed that with the highest tide, the interior base rocks might flood. Otherwise they'd probably remain dry, but for some sea spray flashing.

At the top of the tower, the wall broke in a low jag that might let a climber slip in.

Caius shone the light around the cavern.

Wherever its beam landed, a furtive crab drew away.

Caius trained the light up the cavern's interior wall.

"It looks like we could stay dry in there," said Swift, his teeth chattering.

Without the blanket, the ice of the new night was searing his exposed skin. And his lips were going numb again.

"I can't see many places the water and wind could get in," said Swift.

Caius ran his hands across the stones. "But the rock face is slippery. And very sharp."

Swift looked across the stretch of water to the shore. "Getting inside the cavern seems easier than getting to the beach." He turned his bloodless face toward Caius. "It's our best bet."

Caius studied Swift a moment, then again shone the light through the crevice and examined the cave's dark interior.

Swift peered in again with him.

When the light struck the center of the space, it fell on a pinnacled rock.

"What the…" Caius brightened the beam and swept it up the rock.

At the top of the pinnacle, the light glanced off something shiny.

Swift snatched the torch from Caius and shone the beam at the something.

The beam brightened on a small, wooden box.

A box marked with a silver star.

A Celtic seven-pointed star.

"The Star of Atlantis." Swift spun toward Caius. "It's the freaking Star of Atlantis."

"It might be," said Caius. "But at this point, we can't worry about it."

"We have to go for it."

Swift clapped his hands to wake them, then took two hard handfuls of rock.

He drove the toe of his shoe into a chink and pulled himself onto the rock face.

Caius caught a fistful of Swift's pullover and eased him down. "I know this is difficult for you, but I need your mind off that. Survival is all we should be thinking about."

"What if the Star of Atlantis is something that can help us survive?"

"Swift, I need you reasonable. I need you to help me figure out our next steps."

"Let's get that box, then worry about our next steps."

Caius positioned himself between Swift and the sea, guarding him as best as he could from its sloshing.

"We know that box is here, right?" asked Caius. "And now we know the temper of the cove. We can come back when we're more prepared to deal with the sea like this. We'll collect it when we have climbing gear and a broader boat that can handle this degree of turbulence."

It seemed Caius was trying to make his voice easy. But the

words, pitched to sound sincere, were tinged with a shrill distress.

And in Caius' eyes, Swift read no interest in the Star of Atlantis, in coming back. All he saw was fear.

Swift took his foot down from the rock wall.

He turned his attention to the sea, to their supplies, to their waterlogged boat, to Caius' clothes, and his own clothes, wetting fresh with every striking wave.

"I know that box isn't the priority," said Swift. "But we have to dry off and get warm. We won't in all this spray." He glanced up the rock face, a chaotic uprising of sharp, brittle bulges and shallow, smooth holds. "I know I can climb this."

Despite how perilous the wall seemed, Caius seemed to ease a bit. Swift was speaking from a genuine place of reason, and Caius seemed to sense that.

Swift peeked into the crack. "Weathering the night in there, we'd have a better chance of lighting a fire."

Caius considered the wet stone wall. Ran his hand along it. He slid his fingers into the crevice, sampling the windless quality of the air.

He handed Swift the light. "Here's what we're going to do. You'll hold the light for me, as I scale the wall. It looks like a drop inside of ten feet or so. The base rocks seem broad enough to target. I can handle that. Then I'll help you climb down the inside."

Swift started to nod but paused. Between the two of them, he himself was—without a doubt—the stronger climber. He should be the one figuring out their holds.

It was understood, though, that anytime they got into fixes, Caius was in charge. If Caius suspected Swift of resisting him for the sake of quarreling, he'd get rash and force Swift to cooperate.

The thought of Caius slipping off the wall dropped the bottom out of Swift's stomach.

Swift glanced up at Caius. Wondered what he could say that wouldn't sound like arguing.

Caius studied him. "Out with it. Tell me what you're thinking."

"I should be the one to go first."

"You think you can better find a way up?" asked Caius.

"I know I can."

Caius glanced up the tower, then back at Swift. "Study the holds. Find us a solid course. Once you point it out to me, I'll decide who goes first."

16

Swift paced back and forth along the base of the rock tower.

The wash of the full moon brightened the wall's face, and he could track a clear path to the midway point.

But higher than that, the wall tended sheer.

Once they made it that far up, though, they'd just have to find two or three more holds before catching a low jag at the wall's top. From there, it would be relatively simple to climb over the rim.

He clenched his hands around the heat pack and wiggled his toes.

Caius drew out a pocketknife and cut two lengths from the ends of rope dangling from the knot that held the *Strider*. The spare bits of rope were too short to make use of for climbing. But they would make it possible to carry some supplies into the cavern.

He consolidated their essential gear—protein bars, water, his med bag, bedrolls, warm clothes, and whatever they could spare to burn—into two packs.

He knotted a length of rope to each of their handles, making rough rucksacks out of them.

Swift concentrated on the wall until he felt more sure than not that the footholds he'd spotted were the best ones to go for.

Caius tied the lighter load onto Swift, then strapped the heavier pack onto his own back. He secured the remaining three supply packs against the base of the tower.

Swift glanced at Caius. "This is the path I imagine we'd follow." He ran the light's beam up the wall, pausing at each shallow hold.

Caius spent a moment studying the wall. "All right. You'll go first. I'll stay right behind you, watching what holds you use."

Swift wedged the toe of his shoe into a divot and pushed.

A sheet of algae, slick as grease, slid him right back down.

Caius steadied him.

Swift advanced again on the foothold. He drilled his toe as deeply against the rock as he could, crushing algae, scraping it off. He again tried his weight.

Clearing the hold like that, he could find some purchase on the stone.

He pulled himself a half-meter up.

"Wedge your feet in, as tight as you can," said Swift. "The rocks will hold us if we do that. And the handholds will be easier to grip if I clear them. I'll strip algae off as I go."

Caius studied the coast again, as though hoping that another idea might strike—some way to the beach that they hadn't considered.

But the distance of sea dividing them from the shore stretched what had to be at least fifty meters. And the temperature was plummeting. It wouldn't be long before even their woolen coverings wouldn't fend off the night's chill.

Caius turned his gaze onto Swift. "I know you can do this. I'll be right behind you." He offered an encouraging smile.

The smile looked genuine, but it was certainly contrived.

Swift knew—they both knew—that if Caius slipped, he could crash down onto the rocks, or right into the water. If Swift slipped, there wasn't much chance he'd catch himself. And all his weight slamming into Caius would bring him off the wall, too.

Swift found two new handholds and clung to them.

He wedged his foot into the next hold.

He climbed hand to foot, taking minutes at each hold to clear algae and gain as solid of a grip as was possible. Caius paced himself to Swift, staying exactly beneath him.

Swift tried to not overthink his positioning, but rather threw his focus into seeking the next sharp hold and the next, into trying his weight against each, on placing his feet steadily.

Finally, he touched the top of the wall.

The rim wasn't dry. But it was clear of algae.

"If we can find a way for me to get past you," said Caius from below, "I'd rather drop in first."

Swift shifted a little to deduce if it were possible.

The wall on either side, though, was sheer.

"There are no more holds," Swift called down. "I'll climb in first. I can do it."

He pushed up onto the top of the tower. He laid his chest and belly carefully on a narrow, flattened stretch of the rim.

"Study the drop." Caius handed him the light. "Can you see where you could land?"

Swift shone the light down toward the bedrocks. "The base looks pretty broad. And dry." He traced the light along the length of the bedrocks. "Crabs are everywhere."

"Don't worry about them, they'll scatter once we're down. Shine the light where you plan to land, and they'll likely back out of your way."

Swift brushed the light across the bedrock, chasing crabs from its center.

That part of the floor seemed rather flat and was divided from the rock wall by a gap of only a meter or so. It was close enough beneath where he clung to inspire a reasonable hope that he could stick the landing, square at its center.

"Can you see a way we could make it back out?" asked Caius.

Swift shone the light on the interior wall. "I do. This looks scalable. But to get in, I'd rather chance the drop."

Swift looped the light's cord around his wrist. He eased one foot over the tower's rim, then the other. He lowered himself, dangling over the chasm with two tired arms.

The ache of his muscles, though, seemed to fade, thinking of the Star of Atlantis almost within reach.

He kicked off the rock and let go.

The land was a strike that jarred him, sending splinters of shockwaves up his shins and buckling his knees. It'd felt like jumping from a high branch of a tree and landing on a sidewalk.

"Swift?" Caius shouted.

Swift steadied himself, then eased to sitting. "I'm okay."

He bent and unbent his knees and tried his ankles. They felt shaken but uninjured.

The bedrock beneath him was dry.

He shone the light up at Caius. "It's warmer down here."

"If you have sure footing, don't move an inch." Caius called back. "We don't know what's around you."

Swift shone the light around him. "The rock I'm sitting on is big. It's like an island—the sea is sloshing a few meters below all around."

A progression of boulders crept from Swift's tiny island to the tower wall. They looked passable. Climbing up the inside of the cavern seemed simpler than scaling the outside had been.

And to his left stood the narrow, jetting rock—coned, like a stalagmite in a cave.

Swift shone the light up to its pinnacle.

There, just out of reach—just a short climb away—rested the small box, studded with its glinting Celtic star.

The box seemed very old, like it'd been cobbled with planks from an ancient ship. Swift could make out a metal hinge— tarnished, like silver.

Looking at it, a thrill bubbled up, powering his legs to stand and coaxing a frenetic energy to climb the jetting rock and take its treasure.

But as soon as he was on his feet, the thrill vanished.

At the high mouth of the cavern, easing up to its rim, climbed Caius.

Caius was nothing but a man-shaped shade, backlit by a

scattering of stars in a blue-black sky—cold, and promising the advance of a darkness even deeper, a more terrible chill.

Swift aimed his light on the interior rock wall. "The wall inside here is definitely scalable. I think we'll even be able to climb it more easily. You could scale down it now if you'd rather do that than jump."

Swift stroked the stone wall with the torch's beam, highlighting what steps Caius might take to reach the highest interior rocks.

"Those look steeper than what we just climbed," said Caius. "They seem somewhat concave."

"They're not," Swift called back. "From here, they look manageable."

"Okay, I'm coming down. Shine the light where the footholds look best to you."

Swift swallowed the lump thickening in his throat from the responsibility. If Caius slipped, it would be the fault of Swift's own misjudgment. If Caius slipped...

He removed his pack of gear and laid it aside. "I'll climb the wall first, then I can tell you how."

"No way," Caius shouted down. "Don't take a step." He glanced over his shoulder. "Hang on, my pack is coming loose. I'll have to re-tie it before I try to climb. You sit tight."

"Just throw it down to me," said Swift.

"Forget it. I don't want you moving to try to catch it."

"Then, let me bring you the light," called Swift.

"Don't," said Caius. "The moon's full and rising. I can see well enough."

Caius disappeared from the opening.

Seeing the absence of Caius was far worse than seeing him looming up there, not yet safe.

"Caius?" Swift called.

There was no answer.

Swift shone the light on the tower's wall. He studied it closely, searching out the best path.

Once he spotlighted what seemed the safest course, he

reviewed it over and over until he felt he'd climbed it himself and was confident he could guide Caius down.

He watched the top of the wall. Shone the light at the rim where Caius had been.

The sight of the empty night sky churned an electricity in Swift's chest—the onset of panic.

He stilled himself. Tried to focus on the firm rock beneath him. The absence of wind. The warmth of the heat pack—a slow burn inside of his pocket.

He held still for a long time. A long span of wind howling, of waves smashing the islet, of the light trembling in his tired hand.

Too long.

"Caius?" Swift swept the light across the opening. "Where are you?"

The only reply was a cry of wind and a crash of waves breaking.

Standing on the firm bedrock felt no longer safe but just helpless. The calm that Swift had managed to collect evaporated, spurring his heart to race and making the still atmosphere of the cavern close and choking.

Maybe Caius had dropped his pack. The rope might've snapped, requiring him to climb down and search out another.

Swift lowered the light to a crevice in the rock and tried to peer outside.

He could see nothing but darkness.

He swept the light across the interior of the space.

The light glanced again off the box.

Caius had told him not to move, and that was the wisest idea.

But. What if the Star of Atlantis really was something that could help them?

What if the nomenclature "star" had been chosen for the treasure because it was something that cast light or warmth? It might be some sort of beacon that would flag a fishing boat from way out.

And it would be just a few steps up to reach the box.

The crabs on the pinnacle—red-shelled, pale-faced, blue-clawed little monsters—seemed to be getting used to Swift and were growing bold.

Glaring at him with stalked eyes, they crept into the open.

Swift stepped toward them. "Boo."

Crabs upheaved from every cranny and raced in a hoard to the sea.

The chaos of crabs madly crawling was a terror, but their going cleared a sound way to the box.

Swift approached the jetting rock. He laid his hand on it.

It was bone dry.

Footholds and handholds were easy to find.

This treasure had been his heart's desire for years, but the idea that it might help Caius find his way down, or that it might summon rescue, infused it with a far more poignant worth.

Swift pulled himself up a meter.

He crawled up to the next handholds, earning with diligence every inch won.

Halfway to the pinnacle, he stopped in a cold fear that Caius was at the top of the wall and would catch him.

He glanced up.

Caius wasn't there.

Despite the exhaustion in his hands, despite the terrible vacancy where Caius should be, Swift's fingers felt electric in their itch to touch the treasure box.

Swift kept at his climb, and in a mere moment, he was near enough to the rock's pinnacle to reach the box.

He stretched out his hand—but paused.

What if lifting the box would release some dark sort of magic or curse?

What if removing the box would trigger an earthquake or volcanic fissure that would draw the Kraken-toothed islet into the sea with him in it, with Caius on it?

The notion was foolish, of course, but the idea gripped him strongly enough that he found himself unable to advance.

This islet, this cavern, was the stuff of nightmares, and nothing—no matter how bizarre—seemed far-fetched.

"I found the *Star of Atlantis* book, the map," Swift whispered to himself. "I figured all of this out."

The box, no bigger than a shoe box, looked like a gemstone pronged atop the smooth slate of the rock.

The torch's beam showed the Celtic star to be made of a thick metal, tarnished. Maybe it was genuine silver. Maybe platinum.

Swift drew a deep breath. Touched the box.

He lifted it from its prong and held steady.

There was no tectonic quaking of deep rocks. He heard no scream of a Beisht Kione surging in for the kill; no lyrical laughter of mermaids, come to execute a thief.

Nothing happened.

No noise sounded but the ever-crying wind and the clamor of waves.

The box was just a few kilos and small enough that Swift could hold it against himself with only one arm.

Hugging it, he climbed down to the bedrock.

He shone the light again toward the cavern's top.

There was no sign of Caius.

Swift knelt and set the box carefully before him.

It was fastened just by a catch.

Swift unlatched it. Opened it.

Inside, rested a large, rhombus-shaped cut of crystal. It was pale white and translucent—like a bit of frozen air with cirrus clouds fastened inside.

Swift drew it out of the box.

The crystal was rough-cut on the edges and just a bit bigger than his palm. It was much heavier than it looked, as though it were made of some kind of clear metal.

He shone the torch's beam into it.

Slivers of light scattered around the cavern, blaring on the wall and glinting off the pool below.

Holding the crystal before his face, Swift stood.

"Caius," he called. "You have to see this."

He shone his light along the cavern's mouth.

Caius was nowhere.

17

Swift slid the crystal—the Star of Atlantis—into his pocket.

He stared up to the high wall's opening.

It seemed like hours had passed since he'd dropped into this place. Since he'd last seen Caius.

But time, in this darkness, was difficult to grasp. With the incessant beating of the sea, minutes seemed to creep and quicken all at once—what felt like an hour might've been only a few minutes.

What if it had really been hours, though, since Caius had disappeared?

But it couldn't have been hours.

Still. Where could Caius be?

Maybe a wave had kicked the *Strider* out of her trap, and Caius had seen that and climbed down and was trying to right her.

Maybe he was having some luck.

But if that's what he'd been doing, he ought to have checked in with Swift by now.

"Caius?" Swift called again. "Shout back, at least, if you can hear me."

No response.

At the long silence following, a coldness slipped into Swift's belly.

If Caius had tried to right the *Strider*, and if he'd reached too far, a wild wave could've dragged him under. What if he were drowning, right at this moment? What if he were calling for Swift as he bobbed between the breakers, and Swift couldn't hear him?

With the burst of adrenaline the dreadful vision brought, he stood and shouldered the gear pack. He leapt across a small chasm, over the jostling water, to a boulder leading toward the tower wall.

The boulder was dry and felt steady enough.

Arms outstretched, the heavy crystal weighting his pocket, Swift made his way to the next boulder. The final boulder stood about a meter away from the wall's inner shelf. Between it and the shelf, a few meters down, sloshed the sea.

He leapt the divide.

He landed on the rock shelf and crouched.

"Caius?" he called. "If you can hear me—I'm going to come looking for you."

He ran his hand along the tower wall.

The lower levels were slick with algae—slicker than they'd looked from the bedrock. And everywhere he shone the light, movement flickered—crabs coiling back.

But the higher levels of the rock wall seemed quite dry, and fewer crabs were visible.

Swift fixed his torch in his pocket, aiming its beam at the rock face. He twisted the toe of his shoe into a low chink.

When he put any weight on it, though, he slipped down.

He tried another hold, but it, too, slid him right off.

He tried scraping out the algae, but here it grew in sheets, low and tight, offering little to grip or peel.

Finally, he located a hold that was clear enough to support him. The next holds were a bit simpler to find, but they were shallow and felt risky.

He could be thankful, at least, that Caius hadn't tried this. Climbing down would've been more dangerous than the drop.

"Caius?"

Swift watched the opening, hoping with everything that Caius would appear.

If he did, Swift could tell him to just jump down—that climbing these interior rocks wasn't safe after all.

"Caius—where are you?" he shouted.

He tried to keep his mind off all the terrifying reasons why Caius still wouldn't be able to hear him.

He was busy, that was all. Busy righting the *Strider*. Busy retying his pack. Busy calculating how they'd sail to the coast.

But the absence of any response felt like a verdict. If Caius were anyplace close, he certainly would be answering.

Swift studied the wall stretching between him and the cavern's mouth.

There weren't many footholds higher than the midpoint, and if the ones he'd spotted didn't pan out, he'd struggle to find new ones.

He looked down to where he'd land if he were to fall.

The rocks jetting before the shelf were scattered, but they were more plentiful than the gaps that would spill him straight into the sea.

If he fell, he could catch himself. Probably.

He studied the floor for a landing place in case he had to drop mid-climb.

It'd be smartest to drop to where he'd started from. But the best holds he could see would veer him left. Straight beneath those, the boulders thinned. If he couldn't control his fall, it'd be a straight shot into ice water.

Swift listened a moment for any sound that might reveal where Caius was or what he was doing. Maybe Caius had been calling to him and Swift simply couldn't hear him over the water's heaving.

But in the stillness between waves, nothing sounded but silence.

Swift gripped the rock wall. The sharper edges, chewed by salt and snails, scraped his skin.

But he was glad for it. Rubbing against the rocks made a grating sound that was keeping the crabs at bay.

A pinch from one of those blue claws would certainly rob him of his grip.

Swift eased from one hold to the next, trying not to let his stance widen his pocket so much that the Star of Atlantis could slip out. When he reached the middle of the rock face, he settled into his hold and studied the remaining way up.

No hold within reach, around or above him, looked secure. And he understood what Caius meant, now, that the wall seemed concave from higher up.

He glanced beneath him. He could climb back down.

But the glow that the torch cast downwards was poor. It would be difficult, if not impossible, to feel his way to the holds that he'd come from.

The drop in his stomach at feeling trapped in a climb was a familiar sensation. He'd felt it in trees and on rock climbs before, when he reached a perilous point and had to hang in the middle of a choice where no option seemed dependable.

When Swift was younger and just learning to climb, fixes like this would often paralyze him. Dangling in peril, just crying, usually proved more effective than making any choice.

Because crying would summon Caius.

The old petrification of not knowing what to do—the despair that there might not be any way ahead—was setting in as a heat.

He couldn't let panic take him. Heat rising would mean sweat, and sweat would mean slippery hands. He had to calm down.

He gave the petrification a moment while he held still.

It was a moment of looking down at the distance he'd come; at the sea rocking beneath him—frigid and holding who knew what; of looking up at the distance he still had to go; the apparent baldness of the wall's face.

Minutes passed of Caius' absence, of Swift's muscles tending weaker, of the Star of Atlantis pulling his pocket taut, its corner digging into his thigh; of the torch's beam shining up from his pocket, out the mouth of the cavern and into the dark sky, illuminating nothing.

If he were practicing climbing with Caius, and if he'd gotten into a predicament like this, Caius would tell him to just stay put, to focus on keeping his joints unlocked and nimble, to do nothing rash.

If Caius were here, he'd find a way to help Swift safely drop. Or he'd study the rocks himself and coach him to a safe course.

But Caius wasn't here.

Swift's arms and legs were going cold with his indecision. He couldn't hang on forever. He was in danger, not just of an easy misstep, but of slipping his grip out of exhaustion.

He studied the rock face more intently. He weighed his choices, searching each possible hold within reach, however feeble it seemed. He examined the shape of every divot in the rock face, judging where the stringy algae looked thinnest.

He let himself have just one extra instant of drawing a deep breath, and then it was time. Move up or move down.

The need to find Caius—to see where he was, what he was doing, to see him okay, to find out if he needed help—coaxed a certainty that he should climb up.

Swift eyed his next position and struck out his left hand for a hold.

His grip held.

Managing another precarious grip brought him to a level where the algae tapered, and the next hold was solid.

Swift glanced toward the opening, searching again for Caius coming. But he saw only stars.

Swift could picture Caius climbing on the other side. Perhaps he was stymied, the way Swift had been. But if so, he would've been able to call out, to keep in communication.

From this higher vantage point, the last series of holds were simpler to find.

Swift moved from one to the next until he was less than a meter from the top of the tower. The light gleaming from his pocket, no longer catching the rock, showed him little. He navigated his home stretch more by feel than sight; more by the memory of how this course had looked when he'd imagined a way down for Caius.

Foot by foot, hand by hand, he maneuvered to the top of rockface and pulled himself to the edge of the cavern's mouth.

The moon was fully above the Wentletrap's trees, and it cast a wide blue shine on the distant shore. It was a big moon— bigger than usual at its perigee point.

That moon was a gift. Swift couldn't spare his hand to hold the torch for even an instant.

He eased himself over a divot between two jags at the top of the tower. Clinging to the rocks, he searched the wall for Caius.

Caius wasn't anywhere, climbing.

Swift craned to look down toward the base of the rock where they'd started from.

There was Caius. He was huddling by the bottom boulders, alongside their bundles of gear.

"Oh my God, thank God." Swift eased himself onto the rock wall.

Though he was desperate to finally rejoin Caius, he couldn't let himself move quickly. One false step would mean a fall.

"Why didn't you come back?" Swift hollered. "Why didn't you answer when I called?"

Caius didn't seem able to hear him.

"Did you get the *Strider* out? What were you doing all this time?"

No response.

Why wasn't Caius answering him?

When Swift was nearly down, he risked twisting the merest bit to peer over his shoulder. "Caius?"

18

Swift climbed down the final few meters of the islet's tower wall.

The moonlight was strong, and by its cold glow, Swift could see the holds well.

"I'm coming," Swift called to Caius.

Out in the open air, the wind brought a steady stench of rot from whatever had died in the water.

Finally touching down on the base of the islet, Swift crouched, steadying himself. "Caius?"

Caius didn't respond. Didn't even move.

Swift slipped his shoulders out of the rope binding the plastic pack to him.

"Did you fall asleep?" Swift knelt before Caius.

Caius' eyes were open.

But he wasn't looking at Swift.

"Hey, you okay?" Swift crouched closer.

A gust of wind unbalanced Swift, knocking him back toward the edge of the shelf.

He threw out his hand and snatched at nothing as he caught himself on the rim of the islet, just inches from the sloshing water.

He scrambled away from the drop, then stared at Caius.

Caius hadn't reached for him.

A cold fear in Swift's belly sent ice charging through him.

He crawled toward Caius. "Why aren't you moving? Why aren't you saying anything?"

"Swift," Caius whispered. "God. Swift."

Swift looked closely at Caius. He was sitting up, just like he was resting, with his legs pushed out in front of him.

"What's wrong?"

"Light," Caius managed.

Swift pulled the torch from his pocket and shone it across his brother.

Blood had soaked Caius' right leg from the shin down and was pooling beneath him.

Swift could hardly hold the torch, could hardly stay upright. "What happened?"

Caius managed to look down at himself. "Fell. Leg's broke."

Swift stood, his thoughts racing faster than he could keep up with.

His gaze darted to the dry coast.

Before he'd calculated any solid plan, he was opening their vacuum packs of gear and breathing into them. He tightened their seals and lashed their handles together as tightly as he could.

"You'll have to hold onto me," he told Caius.

Caius turned his head a tiny bit and laid his gaze on the makeshift buoy Swift was strapping to himself. "No way."

Swift knelt and hauled his brother's arms onto his shoulders.

Caius let a scream but didn't resist.

Swift gathered the slack of the ropes and fixed them around Caius' wrists.

He found he could hold the ropes one-handed with Caius draped on his back. With the other hand free, he'd have a chance of fighting the waves, of keeping their heads above water.

He knelt at the edge of the rock, situating Caius' chest firmly against his back. He studied the waves thrashing the rocks at his feet.

After a moment, he'd gathered a loose grasp of the cadence of troughs, coming in short intervals.

He'd have to catch the low point of a wave to keep the water from dashing them right back. It would be a struggle to get beyond these breakers, but if he managed to gain some distance, it looked like the course of the water would eventually change and push them toward the beach.

He glanced over his shoulder. "Hang on."

Caius was silent on Swift's back. A deadweight.

Swift leapt into the sea.

It took mad kicking to struggle away from the islet, and the ice of the water arrested his breath. He didn't realize how much warmth, how much dryness he'd managed to gain until it was vanquished by these frigid waves.

He did his best to work with the water, to use every inch that it gave him, to strain when a wave pulled away from the islet and toward shore.

When he managed to gain four or five meters from the islet, the water quit pushing them back and just jostled them where they hung.

The breakers now tumbled behind them, but here were the swells, and a row of high waves rushed and doused them.

Swift tugged at the ropes and made his way to the surface. Another wave took him, then heaved him back up to bobbing among the blown-up packs.

He wanted to call out to Caius, to hear his voice call back. But each moment out of the water lasted just long enough for a caught breath.

He breathed and sank and kicked and rose. Breathed and sank and kicked and rose. The sequence carried on until his lungs ached and his muscles felt wasted. The iciness of the water seemed to be keeping his body alert, but everywhere skin was exposed, he was losing feeling.

It wasn't until his muscles felt on the verge of cramping that the gravity of what he'd done dawned.

He'd taken his hurt brother into the sea—hauled him into manic waves, with just a few inflated gear packs.

He'd tied the packs well, and the tension on his shoulders, crossing his chest, felt like tentacles snaking.

He pictured air gurgling out of the packs. He pictured the packs weighing down with water and dragging him and Caius together to the sea floor.

Swift flailed in a panic to get loose. He thrashed until his arms and legs felt drained.

Though the packs still clung tightly to him, he'd swatted them loose enough that his head sank beneath the water's top.

Saltwater flooded his mouth and nose, stung his eyes. Gripping Caius' hands was all he could manage as the Celtic waters sealed over him.

His feet would kick, but he wasn't finding the tops of the waves.

He threw all his energy into thrusting Caius away from him, toward what he thought was up. But Caius was tangled tightly to his wrists and couldn't be pushed any higher.

Weakness muted Swift's muscles.

He let out bubbles to ease the pressure on his lungs, but his thrashing demanded air, and his diaphragm spasmed.

Cold water dribbled down his throat.

A blackness rushed him, like a bestial underwater wave.

His limbs went slack.

He couldn't let more bubbles out.

He was barely conscious of the churn of water around him changing tempo when he surfaced against the packs and stayed there. He vomited saltwater and choked down a breath.

The packs were still full of air and floating high.

The wind spinning into him was putrid with rot, but he was breathing, and he could feel Caius breathing on his back.

In the near distance, the coast stretched—a thin line of silver beneath the heavy moon. The current seemed to be pushing them toward it.

Still, that shining sand seemed worlds away.

There was no strategy that would help him reach it. The adrenaline that'd charged him to take on the sea now was drained, and he could do nothing but ride the great waves. If the Celtic Sea wanted to claim them, it would.

He never felt himself drifting to sleep, but from time to time woke in a panic, tearing his face from the skim and choking up the water he'd breathed.

He wrapped the ropes higher around his arms, trying to make the most of the buoyant packs.

He rested his cheek on his shoulder. He angled his body as best as he could to keep Caius' face above water.

19

A return of consciousness.

An awareness of his body, heavy. Of iciness needling his feet.

A heaviness on one side, tugging down his slacks, reported that the Star of Atlantis was still in his pocket.

Its weight felt like the drag of an anchor. Like it was straining toward the deeps of the ocean.

And perhaps he should cast it down. It was by the draw of this stone that he'd coaxed Caius to come here, to this place that'd broken him.

After a few minutes, a sensation of cold numbness muted his sense of the stone.

And it brought some comfort. From his reading, Swift understood what effect cold could have on muscles and blood vessels. He had no idea what Caius had done to himself to cause such terrible bleeding. But icy water might stall the damage.

Glimpsing the coast drawing nearer sparked a glimmer of strength in Swift's senseless legs. He shifted to his side, letting Caius dangle behind him. Positioned like this, he could propel them some.

As he made headway, the rotten smell worsened. Whatever had died must be washing up on the coast.

After a few minutes of maneuvering through swells, he reached a cluster of shallow reefs peeking from the water.

And on their other side—there was the source of the smell.

Moon-white, almost glowing in the water, floated the carcass of a shark.

It at first seemed just a bulk of white, four meters long, a gnawed dorsal fin puncturing the air. But the current was easing them nearer to it, and soon a gape-mouthed face resolved—a sharp-pointed snout.

It was a great white.

An empty socket of eye gazed skyward. The tips of a thousand serrated teeth gleamed.

The carrion birds had mostly vanished, but a few lingered, letting cries as they crossed the full, cadaver moon—its cratered face seeming a mess of bite marks.

Swift peered down to where his legs hung heavy in the water.

Blue sharks trolled the coast of Wales alongside great whites. And fishermen regularly reported sightings of thrashers, like the one he'd seen leap from the water on the night he snuck off in the *Strider*.

And these Welsh coastal waters were ripe hunting fields for tiger sharks—snout to tail, those could reach the breadth of the *Regulus*.

Swift kicked hard, struggling to keep himself from believing that the pressure of water against his legs was pushed from the pass of a circling tiger scout, inspecting the smell of fresh blood in the water.

He kept his eyes on the sallow coast, imagining himself leaving the deep-water canyon, the bedrock creeping up underneath him, slanting slowly to shore.

After a few electric minutes, the cadence of the sea changed, and he felt caught in a drive.

He rode it, letting himself rest when it pushed him, kicking with everything when it sucked him back.

"Caius, hang in," Swift called. "We'll reach the shore, I think."

Caius didn't speak back to him. Didn't move.

Now the rhythm was surge and recede. Surge and recede. Swift quit having to think about swimming, but just moved with the water and dwelt on the warmth of Caius breathing on his neck.

When he was a dozen meters from the waterline, his stiff feet found sand. He tried to walk, but his legs buckled. He pulled forward until his knees hit solid ground. He knelt and unwound Caius' wrists from his.

This shallow water was a few degrees warmer than the cove had been, and in it he gained back some sense of his fingers and toes.

He floated Caius as far as he could, until the gush of the tide spilled them onto a plain of soggy beach.

Swift felt born out of waters. He lay limp, thinking of nothing but breathing, feeling a release from the pressure of water, from ropes constricting his chest.

Caius was lying on his back at Swift's side. His eyes remained closed, but he was moving his hands, clenching his fists as though trying to bring feeling into his fingers.

As Swift lay still, he grew marginally warmer. Finally, he felt he could probably walk, or at least crawl.

Caius let out a weak moan.

That drove Swift quickly up to his feet.

"Swift," Caius whispered. "Pain."

Those words delivered Swift a solid burst of energy, a vision of moving Caius away from the waterline, of putting him in dry clothes and watching him warm by a fire.

He took Caius beneath his arms.

Gear packs dangling from them, he dragged Caius off the soppy sand and onto firmer ground.

This inland beach was baleful—not anything close to a warm fire world, like he'd imagined, but a windswept desolation, stretching and void.

Metallic moonglow draped them, casting a shrill light on the empty landscape.

Here on the bleak beach, the round of the white moon

seemed like no blessing, but the cold shoulder of a sea goddess who didn't care.

Swift searched the vastness of the sand in all directions, looking for any shelter, for any hint of habitation.

There was nothing to be found. The beach was just an expanse of white sand and black tree shadows waving, scraping their crooked fingers against the star-washed midnight sky.

Swift's legs cooperated in hauling himself and Caius, with all their packs, through the thick heaps of dry sand. But this was his final sprint. He kept going, kept pulling, until he reached a cluster of leeward rocks that might guard them some from the sea mist and wind.

He heaved Caius to their center and propped him up against a rock, then dropped onto the sand at his side.

20

Caius' eyes remained closed as he leaned against the rock, and he wasn't holding up his head. But he was breathing steadily.

Swift let himself rest just until he felt like his body was finished coughing up water, just until the woodenness in his limbs softened a degree.

He pushed to kneeling before Caius.

He peeled off Caius' pullover, unzipped his soaked wetsuit, and pulled his arms out of it. He looked Caius over—chest, belly, shoulders, arms.

A series of scrapes striped Caius' side and arm, but they weren't bleeding anymore.

The sand around Caius, though, was darkening red.

Swift's hands were freezing, and the cold wind was sapping almost all his dexterity. He pulled off his own dripping clothes and flung his pullover over the top of the rock. He struggled to twist open the sealed packs.

The cold wind sponged the water from his wetsuit while he unfolded dry clothes for Caius.

Caius lifted his chin an inch and opened his eyes. "I said— no way."

Swift found a towel and tried his best to dry Caius' arms and chest. "I had to be in charge just then."

Caius pawed Swift closer. "Did you choke on the water?"

"I swallowed a lot. I coughed a lot up."

Caius held his hand against Swift's chest. "Does your chest hurt?"

"No, I'm all right." Swift maneuvered a dry wool pullover onto his brother.

Caius' head dropped back toward the rock.

"Hey." Swift supported his neck until he opened his eyes. "You have to be in charge now. I don't know what to do."

"Warm," Caius whispered. "We have to get warm."

"You're bleeding." Swift shone the light on the sand. "Badly."

Caius pointed to his right leg. "Knocked my shin when I landed." He raised his hand to his temple. "Head hurts awful. Is there blood here?"

Swift moved his brother's hand and looked. "No, but it feels swollen."

Caius fingered the swelling. "Has to be a concussion."

"What do I do?"

Caius tugged at his trousers, his wetsuit clinging to his legs. "Find some scissors. Med bag."

Swift drew Caius' medical bag from their supplies and fished in it until he found a pair of scissors.

"Cut the fabric on the inside, away from the wound."

Swift propped the torch beside him on the sand. He did his best to cut through Caius' clothes quickly without touching his leg at all, nor letting the fabric pull.

Caius helped him gently push away his wetsuit and trousers.

Swift shone the light on Caius' exposed leg.

The front of his shin was gashed open, blood-soaked.

And sticking out of the hole was the ragged tip of a yellow bone.

"Caius." Swift, dizzy, caught himself on the sand. "Your leg's ripped wide open. A bone's sticking out."

Caius leaned forward an inch. "Well, bloody hell." He studied the bone. "I knew it was bad. Didn't know this bad."

"Your phone." Swift plundered the pockets of Caius' suit until he found it. He tried to turn it on, but it was shot. "I'll run for help." Swift stood, his legs shaking.

Caius pulled Swift back to his knees. "More important— getting stable." He looked Swift in the eyes. "Concussion. Shock. I'll drift in and out of sleep. I won't make sense. Blood loss. Have to stop that."

Swift laid aside the torch and widened the opening of Caius' med bag. "How?"

Caius absently rummaged until he had his hand on a tourniquet. "You know how to use one of these?"

"You practiced it on me."

"Good enough." Caius placed it in his hand.

Swift did his best to mimic what he remembered Caius doing.

He recalled where on his arms, on his legs, Caius had fixed the band. He remembered the agony of Caius twisting it tight.

Caius cried out.

Swift let go. "Am I doing it wrong?"

Caius felt around the band. "It'll do." He pointed to their bag of provisions. "You eat."

Swift peeled open a protein bar and handed it to Caius. "You have to eat, too."

"Can't. You eat. Get some strength."

Swift wolfed the bar while he dug out their emergency supplies. "We've got rocket flares. Two of them." He presented the flares.

"Don't light them now. No one will come."

"Any decent sailor who sees a flare will respond." Swift struggled to uncap one. "Someone could spot these from miles around. If I launch them straight up—"

"Wait until you see a ship." Caius took the flares from him. "Set those off now, you'd be crying just to the night."

"But your leg."

Swift glanced at the horror of it. Blood was trickling from the open wound, down his calf.

"We have a bit of time," said Caius.

"Until what?" Swift dropped back to crouching on his heels. "Until you pass out and I can't wake you? Until your leg is useless? Until—"

"We have time." Caius' eyes fell shut.

Swift watched his brother's chin drop to his chest, watched the rocket flares slide from his hand.

Swift nudged his shoulder. "Hey."

Caius didn't move. His face had gone the color of the dead shark.

Swift held his hands against Caius' chest until he was sure he was breathing and would keep breathing.

He picked up the torch and studied his brother's gaping gash, his terrible bone.

The seeping blood did look slowed by the tourniquet, but that wasn't such a good thing.

When Caius practiced his skills on Swift, he prattled about what he was doing. And Swift had looked through Caius' texts on trauma medicine and first aid.

There were just basic things dawning on him, but of those basic things, he was sure.

The body needed blood. Without it, Caius' whole leg could be damaged—maybe irreparably so.

The tourniquet seemed to be saving his brother's life, keeping his blood mostly inside him. But if it were, that salvation might come at a price.

Swift pulled Caius' med bag close. "How long can the tourniquet stay on?"

He watched Caius' face. Willed him to open his eyes and direct what had to be done.

Caius didn't move.

Swift searched the med bag, like digging would dredge up the answer.

He found a bundle of antiseptic wipes.

Seawater wasn't clean, and they'd swam through it a long time. He opened a packet of the acrid pads.

Holding his breath to keep his hand steady, he carefully swabbed the skin around the bone.

The shock of what he was doing—clearing blood from an open wound, his fingers brushing layers of fat and muscle—touching an actual bone—was fodder for revulsion.

He kept tabs on his own state, expecting every second to find himself feeling awful, getting dizzy or sickened, the way he felt when Caius cleaned cuts on him.

But he didn't feel anything. His thoughts were clear and flowing quickly.

The tissue he was touching was very cold. Whether from the chilly wind or the tourniquet, or from how much blood Caius had lost, he couldn't judge.

The main thoughts visiting him were questions about when Caius had fallen, how long he'd been at the base of the islet alone, how much blood he'd lost, and whether the tourniquet was doing more harm than good.

Swift shifted closer to Caius, but the sharp edge of the crystal in his pocket—the Star of Atlantis—dug into his thigh.

If it hadn't been for that stupid box, Swift probably would've found Caius sooner. Maybe he would've been with him when he slipped and could've caught him.

Or, if Swift hadn't wanted to go into the cavern at all, neither of them would've tried the climb, and this couldn't have happened.

The Star of Atlantis felt heavy. Too heavy. Like it would slow him. Drown him.

He drew it out and cast it onto the sand.

Caius mumbled something. Opened his eyes.

Swift held up the swab. "I don't think I'm doing this right."

Caius groped for Swift's hand.

Swift dropped the swab and clung to Caius' fingers. "Tell me what to do."

Caius peered down at his leg. "Cleaning it, are you?"

"I should have come to find you sooner." Swift let go of Caius' hand and lifted a fresh swab.

Now, in looking at the gash, at the bloodied gauze, some nausea troubled him.

He swallowed saltwater refluxing, stinging his throat. "I hope I'm helping." He covered the leg with a dry towel.

"You're doing great."

Caius found Swift's hand again and held it.

"You're steady. Maybe you should do this professionally?"

"No thirteen-year-old could do what I'm doing professionally."

Caius smiled. "We're past midnight. You're fourteen. And better ordered than some med students I know."

"I'm not a bit ordered."

Swift uncovered the wound and glanced at it.

"I don't know how much blood you've lost. I'm afraid the tourniquet's damaging your leg, and I've no idea how long I should leave it on. And I don't know if there's anything else I should be doing."

Caius trained his eyes on Swift's. "You got it, didn't you?"

Swift stared at him. "What do I do if the bleeding keeps on?"

"The Star of Atlantis—what is it?"

Swift glanced at the dead-white crystal, heavy on the sand. "If I hadn't gone for it, I might've kept you from falling." He lowered the towel again over the wound. "It was idiotic of me to push you to try out that cave. If I hadn't pressed you to listen to me, you wouldn't have slipped."

"No." Caius closed his eyes. "Nothing you could've done different."

Swift shook him. "I need you awake."

Caius opened his eyes. "Wait for morning. Watch for a ship. Keep yourself warm. Eat. Drink. Try to rest."

"We're not waiting for morning." Swift glanced at Caius' leg, blood seeping now through the towel. "We can't."

"Morning," said Caius. "Morning will show you ships."

Swift glanced at the flares beside Caius, then eyed the cove.

He could barely see the open ocean from here. He'd have to go down the coast some, if he were to have any chance of spotting a ship and hailing it.

Caius pointed at the prism, glistening in the moonlight by his shin. "Show it to me."

Swift dusted sand from the glassy stone and set it in Caius' hand. "I've no idea what it is." He shone the torch on it, scattering shards of light over them both.

Caius smiled some, then winced.

Swift shifted the torch's beam onto his brother's face, his leg. "What should I do? What do you need?"

Caius readjusted himself, then calmed. He seemed more awake, a touch more himself.

He held Swift's gaze. "I think you found a Sunstone."

Swift aimed the light back on the crystal. "What's a Sunstone?"

"Don't know much. Heard of them is all. Bits of crystal Norse sailors used to navigate. Something special about them. They show the way when the way's not plain."

Swift gathered the stone into his palms. "Do you know how they work?"

"God." Caius' head dropped back. "Pain."

The sense of presence faded from Caius. His gaze left Swift; drifted past Swift.

Swift dropped the stone and took his brother's hand. "Do we have any medicine for pain?"

Caius' chin sank to his chest. He stilled, only his shoulders moving with his slow breathing.

Swift gathered the Sunstone again into his palms and sat back on his heels.

He studied it, turning it over and over.

If this was for showing lost sailors the way, he needed it to work. Caius needed Swift to find a way. Badly.

But an old stone wouldn't help him. The Star of Atlantis was nothing that could help him.

He pocketed it. If there was any way to be found, he'd have to find it on his own.

He glanced beneath the bloody towel.

The wound was certainly serious.

But bleeding was a funny thing—just a little could go a long way in seeming copious.

Swift had suffered a bad cut on his forehead and cheek once when he slipped on a rock in a river.

Blood had gushed down him, slathering his face and neck and soaking the front of his hoodie.

By the time he made it back to camp and found his mum, the blood had trickled down his shorts, and even had seeped into his shoes.

Caius had come racing at their mum's screams. He'd snatched off Swift's clothes, stripping him nearly naked.

When he saw for himself the two small sources of the deluge, he'd actually laughed.

He quickly controlled the bleeding and bandaged the cuts, sponging blood off Swift, calmly reassuring their mum, shock-faced—Swift's blood-streaked hoodie dangling from her hand—that there was no danger.

Maybe the red stain around Caius was nowhere near as much blood as it seemed. Swift eased off Caius' shoe and felt his foot.

It was frigid, and the torch showed his whole leg an ugly gray.

If the bleeding looked worse than it really was, maybe he could risk untying the tourniquet.

Maybe he could feed that leg a surge of blood, even just for a minute.

But—manipulating his wound that way might hurt Caius.

He glanced at Caius' face. "Are you awake?"

Caius didn't stir.

Swift unwound the tourniquet quickly. He left it slack on Caius' thigh and shone the light on the wound.

In a minute, the open skin was glistening. A minute more,

and blood was tracing the bone, like a rising tide. Swift blotted away blood and watched.

More came, but the flow was scant.

He packed fresh antiseptic squares around the bone, covered it tight with the towel, then stood.

He backed away, studying Caius' state as a whole.

Caius looked like a stone figure—pale gray. It was like the beach was transfiguring him to be a part of itself. Lithic. Bleak. Bloodless.

The water sloshing near them on the shore, its surge and draw, felt like the aftermath of a world shaken—like a cosmic hand had flicked the planet, knocking it a degree off track.

The sand sticking to Swift's skin felt rougher than he remembered it seeming, the wind colder, the thrashing ocean more hostile.

The stretching beach seemed drawn into metallic shades, like bands crossing a planet's broad disc. Moonlight on the rocking ocean made the sea seem a cobalt expanse; the steely-white waves, thinning and vanishing, shined like other-worldly belts of platinum. Beneath Swift's wet shoes, beneath Caius' bloody leg, the dry sand seemed a muted streak of rhodium.

The waterline of the Welsh coast, the distant dark North Atlantic, the specters of trees looming from the Wentletrap Forest in the east—it all seemed a remnant of an old world, a forgotten world; a world that he barely could recognize.

Here, Swift found he didn't know himself.

He'd always thought of their father as god-like—a Zeus or an Odin. All four of Justus' sons thought of him that way. Odin was the Spear-Shaker, the Chieftain. He was the Wise One. War-Merry. The Father of Magical Songs. The Teacher of Gods.

And Swift had always understood his brothers to be as strong as angels. His family impenetrable.

Brothers weren't supposed to bleed like this.

But Odin, War-Merry—he was also the Father of the Slain.

The empty sea dividing Swift and Caius from their father, from all help, seemed a cauldron of death. The whole place seemed rancid with the carcass, and every mouthful of sea spray it cast was a tincture for drowning.

Dark clouds swallowed the full moon.

Light shrank from the ocean, leaving it a pitching, deep brew.

The northerly gale skidding off the water seemed to spear right through Swift's chest, roaring its bigness in absolute black while Swift perched precariously on his thin band of shore.

He no longer felt like a boy of Devonshire. He no longer felt like Caius' brother. No longer Justus' son.

The sense of lostness drew out only one thing clearly.

If he didn't find some help, the world he'd walk—from this day forward—would not carry Caius.

Swift knelt before the med bag. He cracked open a handful of heat packs.

He slid one in Caius' shirt pocket and nestled the others against his stomach. He unfolded their bedrolls and bundled Caius as well as he could.

He pulled out a sweatshirt and wrapped the leg—no longer gray, but an ugly maroon, the wound still wetting the sand with fresh blood.

Among their supplies, Swift found another, larger torch. Spare batteries were packed beside it.

He dropped out the old batteries, snapped in the fresh ones, then struck the light on. He plunged its handle firm in the sand, clear of rocks, making it a beacon shining like a star toward the sea.

"I'm going up the coast," he told Caius' slack face. "If you wake up and don't see me, don't freak out."

He pulled on a hoodie and tucked a bottle of water and a couple of protein bars into his pockets. He threaded himself into dry windproof trousers and a windbreaker. He picked up the flares and tucked them into his rucksack.

A small first aid kit peeked out from a gear pack. Swift started to load it in with his things but hesitated. If someone happened to find Caius, they might need every bit of first aid supplies on hand.

But Caius had him well trained on the importance of everyone carrying a first aid kit on the coast. He glanced at Caius, then slipped the kit into his rucksack.

He shone his small torch on Caius' face, letting it linger for a last moment.

Caius remained still, his eyelids sealed.

Swift aimed his light toward the roughage at the southern tail of the beach and dashed into it.

21

*S*wift jogged what seemed half a mile along the coast.

Rough rocks and thick undergrowth goaded him more inland, to the edge of the ancient oak forest—the Wentletrap Forest.

The Wentletrap was enormous and thick and notorious for scrambling the senses of even the most capable hiker.

Though a flank of this forest threaded near to their beach house, Swift had never walked even one of its trails. Despite being treacherous with pathways winding and crossing, doubling over on themselves, the entire woodland was somebody's private property.

Swift knew it from maps more than anything, and even if he were lucky enough to find a trail that led anyplace, he'd have to walk dozens of miles to reach the inland side.

It was difficult to navigate even the fringe of the Wentletrap in the dark, as closely grown as it was, Swift having just a small torch.

He was careful to only set foot in it when the terrain forced him that way.

And he keenly avoided anything hinting of a trail that might trick him and lead him astray.

He never stopped but only slowed to a fast walk when he had to catch his breath.

He seemed to be managing a fairly straight course—he ran over and over again into clearings of sand, and the beating of the waves never waned from earshot.

This coastland was showing itself to be as isolated and as sparse as his maps made it seem—too lonely to warrant even a cell tower, much less any village.

If he just kept running, though, maybe he'd get lucky and stumble onto an uncharted house.

A road would be a good sign, but even the idea of finding one seemed to deflate him.

If he spotted a road, how long might he have to run it before encountering anyone?

A vivid mental image struck of Caius alone, propped against the cold rock, his body growing frigid, his leg bleeding heavily again.

Swift hopped into a run.

A sound in the forest, though—something howling—stopped him cold.

It was an animal. Something large, it seemed.

Swift crouched low and watched the dark forest, its gray mist carrying the cry of a creature that he could not name.

It sounded sort of like the cry of a dog, but almost every house in Devon held a dog, and not once in his life had he heard one make such a heart stopping sound.

After a few minutes, the crying died, leaving Swift in a troubled silence broken just by the waves crashing in the distance.

Keeping his eyes on the dark forest, Swift moved on. He expected at every moment to see something hulking and sharp toothed emerge.

He saw nothing, but the longer he stared at the deep emptiness of the Wentletrap's trees, the more terrifying the forest itself grew, and he found himself pressed into a run by a fear that felt primal.

The closer he moved to the coast, the more likely it seemed

that he'd reach a clearing that could reveal the lights of a boat on the water, or the twinkling of a shire, or a road where he might glimpse headlights.

He moved toward the waterline, trudging through thick patches of weeds and damp sand, catching his clothes on burs, tripping on vines.

Finally, the rush of the sea swelled into a swaying cadence of surges beating coastal reefs.

He broke the line of trees and darted onto a wide beach. He studied the horizon, scoured the waves in the distance for ship lights.

The water showed him nothing.

If any ships were out there, they were dark-on-dark. Just invisible shades of sleeping vessels.

Swift peered at the forest. Scanned its trees for any shine.

The Wentletrap was as featureless as the sea.

He swiped his torch's beam around the beach and nearly dropped it as it struck the shape of a man.

A man stretched out on the sand. A man seeming asleep.

Swift started to hurry toward the man but hesitated. He clicked off his light.

He'd noticed no camping gear. A person without gear, sleeping on a cold beach, was off.

This place was unforgiving—anyone crashing on the bare sand here had to be insane. Or a criminal. Or in as much distress as Swift was.

Swift tiptoed over the shadowy sand toward the figure.

From ten feet away, lit just by the cloud-veiled moon, the man seemed to be lying on his back. His hands rested at his sides. It seemed he was dreaming.

Asleep like that, he looked benign.

But you couldn't tell a criminal just by looking at one.

Maybe the man was an escaped convict, hiding from the police. A thief. A serial killer.

Swift clicked on the light but shaded its beam with his hand. He shone the dim glow around the beach.

There was no one else in sight. No shelter. No clear path branching from here to anyplace.

The man twitched and spoke.

"Checkered," he murmured. "Checkered Whelk."

Swift killed the light.

Had the man really said, "Checkered Whelk?" The Checkered Whelk was the ship that Cynfael Maddox captained, in the lore of the Star of Atlantis.

Cynfael Maddox—who was rumored to linger as a spirit on these shores.

Swift crept a step closer to the man dreaming of the Checkered Whelk, to the man whose presence on this savage beach struck so odd that it seemed not unreasonable that he might be a spirit.

In a moment, a soft snoring lilted through the low wind.

It was anyone's guess how many of the legends of Cynfael Maddox were true, and how many were hyperbolic or fiction. But in none of his research had Swift come across any fantasy in which spirits snored.

Swift cautiously drew nearer. He flipped the light on again, keeping it mostly shielded by his jacket. He angled just the edge of its beam on the strange man.

The man's clothes were tattered and dirty, but his face and hands looked washed. His pale hair was carefully braided at the top of his head. On the sides, it was evenly shaved. His trimmed beard was golden and streaked silver as with age, though the man himself didn't look old.

As frightening as was a man lying in the cold, savage open, this stranger might be Swift's only shot at reaching help for Caius. It could be that he was harmless.

Maybe this man was a local out camping, uncomfortable as it looked. If he were a local, he'd know the fastest way to a road or a town.

Swift pressed nearer until he was standing at the man's side. He unsheathed the light and shone it right on the man's face.

The man was muttering again—though, Swift couldn't make out any more words.

On the man's far side, the light fell on a tackle box, a folded blanket, and a fishing pole. In one slack hand, he held a beer bottle. His other hand gripped a long dagger—probably for parring fish.

Swift glanced around the coast, straining to think of any better option.

None surfaced. The only thought that would come was of Caius, gone fish-belly white, his bleeding worsening.

Swift shone the light square at the man's eyes. "Hello?" He bent over the man's face. "Hello, wake up."

The man burst awake and swiped his knife.

Swift leapt back, the knife missing his face by an inch and slashing his clothes, leaving a stinging line across the skin of his chest.

Swift backed away. He glanced down at his torn jacket, at blood wetting it.

He flashed his light onto the man.

"Who's there?" The man guarded his face from the light. "Show yourself."

Swift tossed the light between them, brightening both their faces and catching the shimmer of the knife.

"I'm shipwrecked," said Swift. "My brother's up the coast. He's hurt badly. Can you help me call the coastguard?"

The man struggled to his feet. He was tall—taller than Justus, even.

Swift took another step back.

The man clenched his fist around the knife's hilt and stumbled toward Swift. "Are you a vision?"

The man's eyes were a blue so pale that light seemed not just to glance off them, but to shine from them. The whiteness of the blue struck as ghostly. Vulpine. Fox eyes.

Swift backed off further, clutching closed his torn jacket. "Please. My brother. He needs help." He tripped on a heap of sand and tumbled down backwards.

The man kept on.

Swift scooted away. "I'm only asking for help. Do you have a phone?"

The man, knife in hand, bent over Swift. He blinked a few times.

He straightened and glanced around, like he was struggling to realize where he was. He dropped his gaze onto the knife.

The hilt of the dagger was silver and shaped like a mermaid, its tail twisting around itself. Two diamondesque, sparkling eyes leered beneath the jeweled drops of blood on its blade.

"Seems I laid you a proper strike." The man grabbed Swift by the arm and pulled him to his feet. "What damage did I do you?"

Swift twisted out of his grip, the motion searing his cut chest. "It's my brother. He's broken his leg. He might bleed to death."

The man straightened. "The oldest legends teach that connection—the brightest light—issues from death."

"Please help me call the coastguard."

The man glanced toward Sterncastle Cove, then rested his eyes on Swift.

A strange smile brightened the man's face until he looked like he was on the verge of laughing.

It was as though he were of the race of undying Norse sentries who wouldn't care a thing about a mortal boy on a beach, fussing over so small a thing as death.

The man advanced, crooked a finger into Swift's jacket and pulled it aside, eying the blood on him. "I'm sorry about that."

Swift backed out of his reach. "Look, my brother's hurt terribly. He's in awful pain. Can you tell me where a village is or something?"

The man cracked his back. "You ought not to wake a chap sleeping. Voices and shadows in the dark, to me, mean ambush."

This brand of spouted madness struck Swift as familiar. His grandfather suffered nightmares from fighting in a war. Grandfather had spooked his grandsons many times when the family had spent the night, rushing out of his room and sputtering nonsense about snipers and being infiltrated.

But when awake, he was totally sane.

"When I open my eyes," said the man, "I see comrades falling a moment before I see what's really there."

Aside from the fact that he was holding a knife—stained—the man looked fully sensible. He even seemed gentle, not dangerous—just a troubled soldier, righting himself.

Swift ventured a cautious step forward. "Will you help me?"

The man shifted his gaze from Swift to the ribbons of sea sliding toward them. "I've had not an inkling of luck fishing the shallows tonight. I've dragged up naught but a couple of cod."

"Please, Sir, my brother." Swift gestured behind him. "He's bleeding. He's broken his leg, and he's got a concussion. The night's getting colder. I'm the only chance he has of surviving."

A rush of shock choked off his words. Stating Caius' predicament out loud made him feel the severity, the desperation anew.

"What are you and your brother doing on this godforsaken strip of coast?" The fisherman wiped Swift's blood from his blade. "When the fishing's poor, these waters are nothing but hard-horned rocks and nasty-tempered sharks."

"Look, it doesn't matter," said Swift, his eyes tearing in a lash of gusty wind. "We need a rescue boat."

"You're young to be out sailing these waters. And your accent betrays you as from England's West Country. Whatever drew you to these wilds?"

Swift checked the water again for lights.

"Speak, lad," said the fisherman, "if you want my help."

It seemed, though, that the fisherman wasn't going to help him.

Probably, he couldn't help him.

Swift rounded toward the water.

"Will you not tell me your business?" asked the fisherman.

"I have to find a boat."

Swift walked away.

"I'll help you," the man called. "And your brother."

Swift stopped.

"All you must do is tell me—what business do you have with my waters."

Swift peered over his shoulder. "Your waters?"

How could it possibly matter to him what Swift's business was?

"That's right."

Swift studied him. Whether or not the fisherman was out of his mind, he could have a phone. A lunatic or homeless chap would require a good deal of help himself and must know where other people could be found.

"I'll not stand here forever," the fisherman called.

The sea swaying darkly in the west, its chill, its vast span of desolation—the same raw exposure threatening Caius at this very moment—pressed Swift to play the game.

He faced the fisherman. "We were treasure hunting."

The man let a low laugh. "And what treasure might you have been seeking?"

"The Star of Atlantis," said Swift.

"Many people doubt those legends." The fisherman drew nearer. "Many presume that, if there ever was such a thing as the Star of Atlantis, it's long lost."

"Do you know of it?" Swift discretely pressed his pocket where the rigid crystal lay.

The fisherman glanced at Swift's hand, then looked him in the eyes. "Where's your brother?"

"Up the coast, a mile back or so. He's broken his leg in a complex way. There's so much blood. Do you have a phone?"

"I have a longboat."

"A longboat won't do us any good. We tried to cross the cove in a three-meter dinghy, but it got turned over, and now it's locked against rocks. If we took your longboat, the same thing would happen to it."

"Then I advise you not to take my longboat into Sterncastle Cove."

Swift drifted back a step as the fisherman passed. "You know of Sterncastle Cove?" He followed the man.

The fisherman walked toward a rocky stretch at the edge of

the water. "I know every inch of Sterncastle Cove. I know it as well as I know that stone in your pocket."

Swift stopped.

The fisherman glanced back but kept walking. "Have you any idea what you've found?"

Swift trailed him along the waterline. "My brother thought —I don't know. It just looks like a piece of thick glass."

"That's no piece of glass."

Swift slowed. "It doesn't look valuable or anything, if that's what you're thinking."

"No, it doesn't." The fisherman uncovered a rope, hidden in the sand beneath dry weeds. "Yet, it possesses great value. The Star of Atlantis is a Sunstone—an old block of Icelandic spar. It's an instrument of stellar navigation, fabled to deliver insights, not just to the course of the ship, but to the course of the man."

He kicked sand off the length of the rope. "As legendary as the Star of Atlantis is, so too are Sunstones. They're said to have come from another world, to have been stewarded by ancient seafarers—or starfarers, even."

Swift fingered the edges of the stone through his pocket. If the fisherman decided he wanted it, he could pluck it off Swift, no problem, beneath the threat of that knife.

The fisherman tugged the rope.

From behind a high cluster of rocks drifted a heavy-wooded longboat.

"People have bled for Sunstones," said the fisherman. "Coveted them. Thieved them. Hid them. Lost them. Legends speak of Sunstones aiding in the destinies and fortunes of kings. Of commoners. Of worlds."

It seemed the fisherman, babbling on as he was, might just step into the longboat and sail away in a state of lunacy, abandoning Swift on the shore.

Swift pressed his chest, stinging more now, the blood seeping from it growing tacky and sticking to his clothes. "Can't you just call in a rescue?"

"I can't call anyone, way out here." A smile visited the fisherman. "But not to worry. Legends, for the most part, take care of themselves." He heaved the rope until the longboat drifted into reach.

Swift stared at the fisherman, at the longboat he was towing.

The vessel looked heavy and, though he could sail out west in it, to where ships might wait, it would be tough to control. And it would likely be slow.

"Is there no other way you can help us?" asked Swift.

"You don't need my help," said the fisherman. "You've got that Sunstone."

"What good is it?" said Swift, harsher than he mean to.

But the pain of the cut was growing fierce, and the cold wind was troubling him more. "What I need is a phone."

The fisherman didn't seem to mark the agitation on Swift. He just went on drawing his boat, sweeping its bench clear of sand.

"Looking through a Sunstone shows the moon, the sun, and the stars," said the fisherman, "beyond daylight and clouds."

"A Sunstone"—Swift clasped his pocket—"can show the stars through a day sky? Through clouds?" He wanted badly to draw it out, but he didn't dare.

"Pirates, seafarers, mariners, shamans, and kings all coveted them back before we had navigation inventions—radar and satellites and such." The fisherman gazed from the black thrashing sea to the featureless sky. "Some tellers of tales say that Sunstones are charmed—that the Star of Atlantis holds distilled voices of mermaids—whispers of ancient magic that can summon light from storm-blackened skies." He looked sidelong at Swift. "Could you believe that these waters hold mermaids?"

Swift, his hand clutching his chest, approached the fisherman. "Look, my brother might be bleeding out this second. Could we please hurry up with readying the boat so we can find a ship I could hail?"

The man stood tall and folded his arms. "Ask me if I've ever seen a mermaid."

Swift just stared.

"Go on." The man's expression was merry. "Ask."

Swift glanced back toward the beach where he'd left Caius.

This was carrying on too long, but he could think of no other way forward than to indulge the fisherman's whims.

Swift asked, "Have you ever seen a mermaid?"

The fisherman flashed a grin. "No."

Swift threw up his hands. "What are you playing at?" He gestured north. "My brother."

"Lore is one thing." The man closed in on Swift. "But the question—your question—has naught to do with any myth."

Swift froze as the fisherman, gazing at the blank sky, laid his hand on Swift's shoulder.

"The question is," said the fisherman, "what manner of strange really is out there?"

Swift stared up at the fisherman. As crazy as his talk was, Swift felt as though he really kept secrets.

The fisherman offered him the longboat's rope.

Swift took the rope but hesitated to move out from under the fisherman's hand.

"What's out in the great beyond is wondrous." The fisherman's eyes narrowed. "And treacherous." He ran his gaze down the split in Swift's jacket, his gash still leeching warm blood. "Understand that, by claiming the Star, you're pinned with a role in this magnificent mess. We both are."

Swift glanced at the longboat. "Can we go?"

The fisherman backed off. "Be mindful to keep your eyes peeled, lad, not just for hidden stars, but for hidden worlds." He stared at the breakers, then further out, toward the bleak horizon. "You'll do well to remember that the real is always more fantastic than the imagined. Not unlike that Star, now asleep in your pocket."

This man seemed more than a mere fisherman. With his height, with his oracle-sounding speech, the way he was young-seeming and old-seeming all at once, with his rare knowledge of the Star of Atlantis, it felt like he was more than a man, even.

It was like he was posted here to watch over the Star of Atlantis; a protector, like in Norse myths—a protector of ice and fire worlds who'd someday cut down everything with his red sword at the falling of the twilight of the gods.

"Who are you?" asked Swift.

The fisherman kept his vigil with the sea. "I'm exactly nobody."

Swift gathered the rope and waded into the water. "You don't have a name?"

"Those who don't need names don't use them."

Swift heaved at the rope until the nose of the boat wedged into the sand. "When you were sleeping, I thought you said something of the Checkered Whelk. What do you know about it? Do you know the history of the Star of Atlantis?"

The man's smile was old. "I know many secrets of the sea."

A shrill howl—the howl that Swift had heard before—pealed again.

This time it rang closer. More sharply.

Swift and the fisherman together stared behind them at the Wentletrap Forest.

"What was that?" asked Swift.

The fisherman scanned the forest. "A summons."

His words sent a chill through Swift.

Whatever was making that cry sounded vicious. And if that was a summons—what could it be summoning?

Swift stared again at the water.

As treacherous as the Celtic Sea was, it seemed familiar, at least—a creature that he understood.

That ringing cry seemed an unrecognizable kind of savage. Other-worldly.

Swift gripped the longboat's rim to steady her. "Maybe you should climb in first?" He glanced back.

The fisherman was gone.

Swift spun. "Hello?" He swept his torch across the beach.

There was no sign of the fisherman. Even his gear was missing.

"Hey, aren't you coming with me?" he called to the darkness.

No answer came.

Swift stared at the empty beach, scanning it for any motion, for any hint of where the fisherman could've gone.

There was no voice on the wind. There were no footfalls.

It seemed he'd simply vanished.

Swift turned toward the sea—the black, heaving sea; toward the black, cloud-thickening canopy pressing the west.

He drew the Sunstone from his pocket and held it to the apex of the sky.

He jolted at the shock of light points manifesting—gentled stars that clouds were obscuring, captured in the heart of his stone.

Peering through the Sunstone, Swift scanned the horizon.

Through it, the night sky was dazzling. Even the water flickered with tendrils of moon and starlight drifting from beyond the cloudbank.

He lowered the Sunstone and studied the longboat, large and clumsy and jostling.

Its dark, wide wood bespoke a heaviness Swift could feel in his wasted legs. It had no rudder, no sails. Just two thick oars.

A skilled rower like Justus might be strong enough to pull this longboat alone and control its heading. That fisherman certainly could, as muscled as he was. But no lad could, even if he had turned fourteen tonight.

And as wondrous as the Star of Atlantis was, it was nothing that would help him fight the sea with those two heavy oars. Especially with the way that his cut chest was stinging.

Swift gripped the Star of Atlantis—full of its secrets of light —the treasure Caius had brought him here to claim—Caius, who was alone on the godforsaken shore of Sterncastle Cove.

Swift had no choice but to try to manage the longboat. To try to reach the open water where a ship might be found.

With the guidance the Sunstone might lend—if he could control the longboat—he'd be able to keep true to west. He could aim for the tracks of the North Atlantic where night-fishing boats were most likely to drift.

And if he could locate a current, maybe that would pull the boat fast enough to let him sight a ship on the water, hours before daybreak would show him one.

"Come hell." Swift heaved the longboat into the draw and

leapt in. "*Come storm waters. Come the Kraken.*" He stowed the rope in the stern and unhooked an oar from portside. "*I'll forsake all sound shores for the night-lighted passageways— untrodden reaches—for sun-brightened visions, for insights of stars.*"

He barreled into the crash of waves.

22

*S*wift had no sense of time as he fought the current.

All the fury of the deep North Atlantic seemed to be pouring in, heaving the water into high waves.

Difficult stroke after difficult stroke, he eased further from the coast.

A savage pain lashed his cut chest with every pull, but after a while, the discomfort got lost in the burn of his muscles. His arms, still exhausted from swimming, tired quickly. But he forced them to move, even if his pulls were weak.

He gave himself moments of rest, but only when he absolutely had to. When he stopped rowing for even a second, it seemed the sea reclaimed meters of water he'd crossed. And when he picked up the oars again after a pause, his knife slash smarted ever more sharply.

He pulled the longboat forward until he felt a catch on the hull—the arc of a gripping current.

Swift let the draw have her.

A few moments of stomaching steep waves delivered him to drifting in a field of gentle waters.

He scanned the sea all around.

There were no lights. No ships.

From here, he couldn't even estimate where the deep sea finished and where the coastal waters began.

He pulled his torch from his rucksack and shone it across the deeps.

Justus often talked of the deeps, of their mystery and wonder.

"The deeps" had always seemed abstract—but at this moment, Swift understood them.

There was nothing but deep blackness above him, deep stillness around him, deep water beneath him.

"The deeps" seemed to be what he might call the concentric waves of disturbed waters rippling from the boat into more and more profound volumes of emptiness.

And at the moment, the deeps were carrying him, a gentle current moving the boat.

Swift laid down the oars.

Finally at rest, he grew fully aware of how much his chest hurt.

He unzipped his jacket and tried to steal a look at the cut, but the boat set to rocking, the heave of a cross current striking.

The boat seemed to be angling off course.

Swift drew his Sunstone from his pocket and raised it to the apex of the sky.

He peered at the shimmering night, scanned the starfield until he found Orion teetering at the brink of the western horizon.

A quick estimation of the angle of the longboat's bow beneath Orion told that the current was tweaking him south.

He needed west.

If he drifted south, he'd remain too near to the coast and would have less chance of spotting a ship.

And, if worse came to worst and he didn't find a boat, a southern current might draw him far away from his starting point. If that happened, he'd never have the stamina to make it back to Sterncastle Cove. Back to Caius.

West, it had to be. But without sails, he'd have to fight the waves to maintain his heading.

He searched the sky for Mintaka—the highest star lighting Orion's belt, almost true to west when it set.

Through the Sunstone, he spotted Mintaka, hovering just above the horizon, lighting the curves of the waves.

Swift cut a line in the sea, striking it hard, peering through his Sunstone when he had to rest, until bright-blue Mintaka was piercing his stone in radiance, straight over the tip of the bow.

He paddled until there was more of a glide and less of a struggle in keeping him true to Mintaka's shine.

The wind was soft, and shallow waves nudged the boat but didn't set it off course.

Swift rested the oar on the bench and tracked Mintaka with his Sunstone until he was certain he was consistently coursing due west.

Gliding on easy waters, silent but for the gentle slosh of waves brushing the hull, the bite of his knife cut swelled.

Swift pulled near his rucksack and dug out the small first aid kit.

He shifted to sitting in the boat's bowl and balanced the light on the bench before him, angling it on the center thwart until its beam brightened his chest.

He pulled aside the tear in his clothes.

The knife cut was long, stretching in a diagonal gash from his left clavicle to the inner base of his right ribs. The skin around the cut was swollen and felt warm.

It'd been foolish to stand so close over the sleeping fisherman. If he'd stayed back just a few inches more, this wouldn't have happened.

He couldn't help but feel lucky, though, that this wasn't worse. If he'd been an inch closer, the knife would've cut deeper. Or it might've caught his face and neck.

The cut appeared shallow, and the bleeding had stopped. But the taut skin on either side was erupting into blotchy patches that were spreading around his ribs.

The pain of it was fierce when he twisted, and the blood-stained skin was terrible. But even so, it seemed a trifle after what he'd seen on Caius.

He opened an antiseptic swab and did his best to clear off the tacky blood.

The lightest touch with the wipe set the cut to brutally burning, though, and he had to stop over and over to catch his breath.

When he'd used up two swabs, he angled the light more directly and examined his progress.

He'd only managed to clean off the blood a few inches down. And he hadn't been able to stand to touch close to the center of the cut.

If Caius were with him, he would've made Swift lie still and take the pain until the deed was done. And so he held his breath, opened a fresh wipe, and swept it along the swollen line.

He screamed, tears dripping down his face, but he made it through four swipes.

When he was finished, even the brush of the air and the motion of his shallow breathing was excruciating.

Drawing air in just agonizing bursts, he searched inside the first-aid kit until he found a tube half-full of lidocaine-laced antiseptic ointment and a couple of strips of gauze.

He held the tube above the cut, starting at his ribs.

The greasy salve didn't hurt, but the waves were jolting the boat, and keeping his hand steady was impossible. It felt like the tip of the tube was another knife's point, every jerk slicing him over again.

He'd just made it halfway up the length of the cut before the medicine was spent.

Shivering with the cold of tears on his face, with the night wind needling his bare chest, he pressed gauze squares to the wound where they would stick.

He used bandaging tape to fasten his hoodie and jacket tightly around him, to hold everything in place without having to lay sticky tape on his irritated skin.

The hoodie pressed a soothing warmth.

Swift cracked open two heat packs to make the most of the effect. He dropped them into the hoodie's front pockets.

He leaned against the boat's stern, letting his weary back rest.

Hands shaking, he lifted the Sunstone again to the horizon.

The boat had again drifted south.

He tolerated knowing the boat was off course long enough to eat a protein bar and drink half a bottle of water.

Holding his breath against the sear of the troubled cut, he sat up again on the bench and wrestled with the sea until the Sunstone showed him that he was slipping in the upsweep of a silky west-tending current.

The ointment seemed to be doing some good, muting the pain where he'd managed to lay it.

But nausea swelled from the agony of moving, and a leaden drowsiness struck.

This drowsiness wasn't a casual need for sleep at a late hour, like the somnolent feeling of staying up late. This was a lethargy that threatened to put him out the way Caius was out. It was the exhaustion that came with a fever.

Swift peeked beneath the gauze strips, at his cut.

Purple pinpricks were speckling him now, all along his front and sides.

Could that knife have been poisoned? Had the fisherman used it to clean a blowfish or venomous eel? Maybe the fisherman hadn't washed it in weeks.

Swift lost his bearings a moment and felt he was falling. He had to grip the sides of the longboat to steady himself.

In all this black sea and black sky and black mist, it seemed he might've wandered into the deeps of oblivion, with nothing above him, nothing below.

He seemed to be levitating in a state between drowsiness and restlessness, seeing nothing but black whether his eyes were open or closed.

This nothingness of the North Atlantic seemed the worst of its monsters.

In that blank stillness, his body now shivering, a dark truth dawned.

As strong and solid as his life felt, it was fragile.

He wasn't invincible, and neither was Caius.

And this was their last night.

Caius would be dead within hours, frozen or septic, and Swift himself would soon follow.

Why had he thought he could get anyplace in this longboat? Once he realized that the fisherman had abandoned him on the beach, he should've gone back to Caius.

If he'd trekked back through the rough, back to Sterncastle Cove, neither he nor Caius would have to die alone.

A brightening in the sky—clouds thinning and sailing away —unveiled a starscape that glistened on the sea.

All those stars, all that light, seemed to beckon him, seemed to rally him to think not of oblivion, not of the swallowing sea, but of a ship that might be, right now, drifting just out of sight.

Swift tried to force himself up to sitting on the bench—but with the cut's searing, he couldn't straighten.

After struggling a few minutes, he gave into the draw of the longboat's curving stern and rested against it, his head propped on his rucksack.

Swift lifted his Sunstone and traced the brightening stars, thickening into the band of the Milky Way.

He scanned for anything dark on the horizon that might break their glow—the needles of masts, the bulk of a broad hull, the stacked squares of sails. He watched the west until his head ached and he had to rest his arms.

Lying in the cradle of the boat, lilted by the water, hearing nothing but the slosh of tiny waves, Swift felt part of these deeps —wild and darkly peaceful, as full of waiting terrors and sleeping monstrosities as anything he'd read about.

A Kraken hadn't sunk the *Strider*, but it might as well have.

The Cthulhu hadn't dragged Caius off that rock, crunching his leg and jagging his tibia from his skin—but the fall he'd suffered had been just as horrific as if it had.

Swift had left Caius alone in a nightmare, concussed and propped on a hard rock and in terrible pain, with no relief but a loss of consciousness; lonely in the cold of night; bleeding, his leg useless; maybe having lost too much blood to recover.

The chase of the Star of Atlantis felt like the ultimate fool's errand.

And Ash had pressed him into this.

Ash—who blamed Swift for their old accident. Ash—who harbored enough hate for Swift to have told him to go to Hell.

Ash—who might get his wish tonight.

The blind water carrying the longboat seemed as cruel as Ash. How could the North Atlantic, so quiet now, feign peace when its terrors might be killing Caius?

If Caius died, how could Swift ever love the ocean, ever come to the Celtic again? How could he read about the North Atlantic's mythic monsters if Caius lay in a graveyard because of the real ones?

Swift found he couldn't bear such thoughts long. Nor could he manage to hold his eyes open to anything more than slits.

He managed to raise his Sunstone again to the western sky.

The light points brightening inside its crystal served as a small assurance that there still were stars—suns that, for thousands of years, had risen as celestial lighthouses, pointing to sailors the way home.

Swift's hand fell to his side, the Sunstone fixed in his grip. His eyes closed. His mind drifted to the fisherman and his knife.

The cut ached at the memory of that shining blade—just a flash of silver like the flick of a fish's tail, and then dark with warm blood.

The fisherman had known about the Star of Atlantis. How that could be?

Swift's research had yielded hardly an inkling of where it was, and nothing about what it was.

Yet that fisherman had known.

And the fisherman knew Swift had taken it, and he let him. He gave Swift his boat. He told him how to use a Sunstone. And then he vanished, like he'd never been there at all.

Like Swift had imagined him.

The longboat jumped as a mountainous wave surged.

A wave with that much energy might've been heaved by a nearing boat.

Swift pushed to his elbows, holding his breath until the pain of moving ebbed.

He held up his Sunstone and scanned the water.

The Celtic was empty at all points, except when he steadied the Sunstone just to the right of the tip of the longboat's bow.

Holding it there, it was like a sheen of light hung over the swells.

He lowered the Sunstone and studied that patch of water and sky.

To his naked eye, everything was absolutely black.

He again lifted the Sunstone and gazed through it, left and right.

Again, at that single place, just off starboard—there, a pale light shone. It was like a white comet, hazy, hovering over the top of the sea.

Cloud-shrouded starlight and moonlight might be filling a ship's sails, way out there, with the invisible light that his Sunstone could catch.

Swift held his breath against the fire in his chest as he eased onto the bench. He lifted the oar from the side of the boat.

The pain was horrendous, but once he'd born it a minute, the shock passed, and he found he could deal with it.

He paddled toward his new heading—a few degrees northwest.

He felt he was handling the pain well, until he tasted blood and realized he was biting his lip to cope.

He kept up with his paddling, switching from side to side every few strokes, until he was sure that he'd managed some distance.

He laid down the oar and lifted his Sunstone.

The light was still there. But closer.

Swift reached again for the oar, but the effort delivered a wallop of pain that left him dizzy and sweating.

He tried again to grasp the oar but slipped off the bench and couldn't maneuver back onto it.

Swift dug into his rucksack and pulled out a rocket flare.

He eased onto his back, his glazing eyes staring at cloud-shrouded stars. He put all his effort into twisting the caps off the flair and setting the trigger.

He fired.

The flare brightened and leapt in a spiral, straight up into the black. It burst like a spray of blood.

His duty done, Swift sank back.

Blinking tears from his eyes, he gazed at a new brightness flickering, hovering at the bow of the longboat.

Something was here, in the boat with him. Something shimmering.

Swift managed to push to his elbows.

There, leaning back against the bow of the longboat, sat Caius.

"It isn't real," Swift heard himself whisper. "Caius, you're on the coast."

But it felt real. Even when he closed his eyes, he sensed Caius near.

Maybe Caius really was with him somehow. Maybe Caius was dreaming of seeing him, too.

With the sense of Caius in the boat with him, Swift finally felt he could relax.

Caius would keep them true to that glow drifting nearer. He'd manage the heavy oars and difficult currents and would watch over Swift.

Swift tried to move, to see the Caius specter more clearly.

But the motion roused a bombardment of pain.

And on its heels came a terror that Caius finally had bled out and died; that he was a spirit now, come to haunt the North Atlantic.

Maybe come to claim Swift, too; to usher him into the deeps where wander the souls of people who die on the sea.

23

Far-off voices, shouting.

The words were tinted Scottish.

Swift forced open his eyes and found the sky clearing. Stars were winking between hazy clouds.

He lifted his Sunstone and focused on the bare, bright stars.

Through the Star of Atlantis, stars were more than stars.

They were suns. Brilliant, spherical, warm, drifting. They had dimensionality. Curvature. Even rays. It might've been a trick of refraction, of shards and halos pronounced by veins in the crystal. But maybe it was real.

"The fisherman thought so," Swift heard himself saying. "Hidden stars. Hidden worlds."

The voices grew nearer, swept over the water, like beams of light coasting and filling his stone.

Swift called, "What if Sunstones bring out the truth of the stars?" He pressed his ear to the sky for a response.

There was no response.

Maybe there was nothing out there. Maybe that glow on the horizon hadn't been starlight gleaming on far-off sails, but a concoction of fever.

As wakefulness faded, the Sunstone slipped from his fingers.

More voices. Or hallucinations of voices.

The longboat jolted, like someone had dropped into it.

Swift tried to move, but before he could summon any strength, someone was scooting along the bench and pulling him to sitting.

He let a cry, but the pain seemed delayed, striking what had to be seconds after he'd been moved. There was splashing in the water behind the voice and the tremble of an engine.

"And where have you come from?" asked the voice.

Swift stared into the eyes of a man staring at him. "Hell and dark waters."

"I don't suppose you could be more specific?"

Swift tried to make out the features of the man, but they faded to dimness behind a bright light.

"It's a boy," the voice called toward the splashing. "There's blood on him."

The man set aside the light and tore the tape off Swift's clothes. He slipped Swift's jacket off him and spread open the slash in his hoodie.

A fearful look darkened his face.

Swift glanced down at himself.

The scarlet welts, rising largest along the line of the cut, blazed hot-red at the edges.

"What on Earth did that to you?" asked the man.

"Fisherman had a dagger," Swift said. "Fought in a war, I guess. I wasn't an ambush or anything. I just wanted to say —'hello, wake up.'"

Another clunk, like someone else had landed in the long-boat. "Let's see him."

The first man lifted Swift, shifting him like a small child into the lap of the other.

"I'm fine, I'll oar." Swift forced. "Mintaka keeps the west, and I can see her in my stone."

"You'll lie still," said the second voice, more heavily brogued than the first.

Eyes barely open, Swift watched the first man lash a rope to the bow of the longboat. The man caught a bundle that someone tossed down.

Someone cut open Swift's hoodie and wetsuit. They lifted a soapy wet rag and bathed his chest.

Swift couldn't draw breath.

"Can you tell us your name?"

He knew only agony, white and shining, blinding him, leaking tears down his temples.

The man let up. "Lad, your name."

Pain receded like drifting clouds unveiling stars.

"It isn't about me," Swift forced, the words seeming cotton-mouthed and hot. "It's about my brother. On the beach beyond Sterncastle Cove. There's a bone sticking out of him."

"How far is the cove?" The man stretched a cloth over the cut. "Can you describe it?"

Swift tried to push the man's hands off, but more hands advanced and restrained him.

"We need it." Swift pawed the baseboards for his Sunstone. "This." He lifted it. "I left a light by my brother. It's nothing that can keep him warm. Not a lick of light besides—just a dead shark, cold white in the water. That's a kind of moon. Bone crushing rocks—then we swam."

"Quick to the coast, then track it," called the man, above the splashing. "Look for any light on the beach. Might be inside a cove."

"Take it." Swift forced the Sunstone at him. "It shows you the course, okay?"

The man received the stone. "That's enough from you, now. Close your eyes."

The longboat jerked as the tow line pulled taut, then glided in the wake of the big ship.

Swift's head fell back against the man's arm. "Caius is out of blood."

24

Swift woke to the roar of an igniting engine.

He found himself shivering, propped against a cushion, leaning on a wall in the interior cabin of a sailboat.

A bright morning sea frolicked outside a wall of tall windows, the waves shining blue in a radiant dawn. The boat was lilting, but it didn't seem like she was cruising.

Beside him, Caius was lying flat, strapped to a carrying gurney.

They both were wrapped tightly in blankets.

"Caius," Swift whispered.

Caius didn't respond. He was gray and looked colder than Swift felt.

His leg was propped on a cushion, the wound and bone bound. His bare foot sticking out was a sickening cross between yellow and blue.

Swift tried to sit up more. An aching in his head slowed his moving, but he managed to struggle to his knees. Beneath the blanket, he was stripped down to the waist.

Despite the chill in the air, he shrugged off his own blanket and tucked it around Caius.

Thoughts weren't coming easily, though, and by the time he

was satisfied with his work, Swift found himself mortified, wondering whether he'd just wrapped a corpse.

A medic in blue scrubs knelt before Swift and spoke.

Swift focused on his face and tried to understand, but the medic's voice came at him as though they were underwater.

A woman in nursing scrubs came, and the two of them together carried Swift to the other end of the cabin where a white bed waited.

The medic needled an IV into Swift's arm, then flicked on a light that shone on his cut chest.

A grave expression traced the medic's face as he studied the cut.

"This might sting"—the medic lifted a cloth wet with yellow-brown fluid—"but it'll help with the pain." He set to swabbing the cut.

The agony summoned screams from Swift, but the medic didn't let up.

Swift tried not to cry but stopped worrying about it when he realized his body was too dry to push tears.

The fluid from the IV was chilly enough to shiver him, but it seemed laced with something quickening, because in a moment, he felt wired, like he'd kept himself up all night on hot coffee, his mind racing, his eyes hardly able to blink.

Whatever the medic had spread on Swift's chest seemed to mute the pain some, and the agony of breathing diminished.

"Now that's a mite better," said the medic. "Seems you're a bit more wakeful."

"I have to be by him." Swift winced as the man dabbed again at the cut. "Even if he's gone."

The medic smoothed a strip of gauze over Swift's chest. "What's your name?"

Swift looked him in the eyes. "Is my brother dead?"

"No, lad. Someone very brave must've tended him."

He pushed something into the IV.

"We found him warm and sleeping, his leg doctored as well as might be, given the circumstances."

Swift relaxed with the fading of pain.

The medic looked kindly at him. "How about a name? Can you tell me your name?"

"Swift Kingsley." He tried to sit up to see Caius better, but he didn't have the strength. "Did you see Caius' leg? There's a bone out of it. He lost so much blood."

"That he did. But we put more into him. Caius will need surgery for that leg. As soon as we dock, you'll both be off to the trauma hospital in Bristol."

The medicine the medic had pushed seemed to be hitting more strongly. Tension was draining from Swift's muscles.

"We found enough information on Caius to help us get in touch with your brother—Edric. But no one's had luck reaching your parents."

If Justus and Mum were out of touch by phone, Edric probably wouldn't know how to track them down.

"They're on holiday, in France," said Swift.

"Did they tell you at which hotels they might be staying? It appears they didn't leave that with Edric."

"No, but..." Ash's father, Mr. Emberly, was keeping an eye on the house. Edric probably didn't know that.

The last person Swift wanted to think about now, much less contact, was Ash.

But Mr. Emberly would have Justus and Mum's travel plans. He could trace them faster than anyone.

"I can give you a number to try—it's a neighbor who's looking after our house."

The medic handed him a paper and pen.

Swift managed to write Mr. Emberly's number.

"The boat I was in—it belongs to a fisherman," said Swift. "He'll be wanting it back."

"You said as much while asleep. Which brings us to the matter of—what manner of trouble did you wander into during the night? From the speaking you did, it seems there was a ghost fisherman, a drowned pirate, and a mermaid with a knife."

"I don't know about pirates and mermaids," said Swift, "but there was definitely a fisherman. And a knife."

The medic checked Swift's IV, then settled onto a stool. "I'd like you to think very hard and try to tell me exactly how you got that cut."

A coolness on Swift's thigh brought his hand to his trouser pocket. There rested the Star of Atlantis.

"The fisherman was sleeping," said Swift. "I didn't mean to surprise him. He talked about mermaids and legends of stars and about ambush troops."

"Sounds like you had some wild dreams." The medic lent an easy smile. "Not to worry, though. It's no wonder with your fever. I've given you plenty for the pain, plus medicine to cool you off. In a bit, you may have a better sense of what happened."

"But I know just what happened," said Swift. "I found a fisherman. He gave me his boat, and he talked of sea legends. I'd swear by it. And anyway"—Swift touched the edge of his bandage—"how else could this have happened?"

The medic waved Swift's hand away from the gauze. "Best I can tell, you dropped down a sharp boulder. Or you stumbled on the beach and picked up that cut from a bit of nasty waste in the sand. You've landed yourself a terrific infection."

"My cut looks straight, though," said Swift. "Straight as a blade. A cut from a rock would look jagged."

"Any manner of metal on the beach could make a cut like that."

Swift focused on the medic. "This came from a dagger."

The nurse approached, holding a phone. "We reached the neighbor who can get in touch with your parents." She held out the phone. "Do you want to talk to him?"

The thought of Mr. Emberly brought a wash of comfort. He wasn't at all cruel like his son. Rather, he was one of the kindest people Swift ever had known. He'd certainly do everything he could to find Mum and Justus.

Swift reached for the phone. "Mr. Emberly?"

"Swift?"

The sound of the voice dropped the bottom out of Swift's stomach.

"Swift—it's Ash."

25

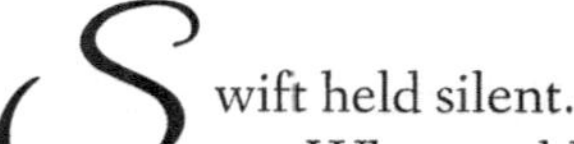wift held silent.

What could he say to Ash?

Was there anything he could say to a person who'd driven him to a place he'd almost died? To a place Caius had almost died.

He should just hang up.

"I know I'm the last person you want to talk to," said Ash. "But hear me out."

Swift couldn't bring himself to speak. But neither could he bring himself to hang up.

"We know you and Caius were in a bad accident," said Ash. "Edric got in touch with my father already. He's working to find your parents. And I promise you, he soon will."

Hearing Ash's voice brought a touch of comfort that surprised Swift. It was Ash, yes, but—Ash being gentle in a way Swift hadn't felt in five years.

Still. This could just be Ash reeling him in for a strike.

"They said that you guys wrecked the *Strider*," said Ash. "That's awful. I'm so sorry that happened."

"Are you?" Swift gripped the phone. "When you sailed off, standing on that leviathan ship that you rented, I saw what you did. I got the message."

Ash was quiet a moment.

"I'm not proud of what I did," said Ash, "renting that brigantine just to get under your skin. Right after my ship pulled away from you and Caius, I felt terrible."

"Then why did you do it?"

"It's sort of hard to explain," said Ash. "I've just always been so angry at you for our accident. So jealous, too, I guess. You've always been the stronger one. The smarter one. I see, now, how mean I've been. Because of the jealousy."

"It wasn't jealousy that made you act the way you have," said Swift. "That's been a choice."

Ash let those words ring. And then—"I guess you're right."

Swift startled at the admission.

"It's just—when we were small," said Ash, "you used to do everything I'd tell you, and it felt good."

"So you were kind to me as long as I did what you wanted?"

"No, that's not it," said Ash. "I don't know. When my mum left, it was like no one listened to me anymore, or did anything I wanted. But you listened to me."

"If you liked having me as a friend so much, why would you take out the Tumble on me? And why did you push me away?"

"I guess," said Ash, "because you were getting better than me at everything."

"That isn't true. You're the athlete. Everyone at school wants to be friends with you."

"No, they don't," said Ash. "But besides—you don't care about what anyone thinks. It's just one more way you handle yourself better than me."

That wasn't exactly true. As much as Edric, as Caius had coached him to follow his own heart, everyone else be damned— Swift still cared what Ash thought.

"I admire that about you," said Ash. "I've always admired you. But instead of telling you, I—"

"—pressed me into a competition that almost killed me and my brother?"

"You have a right to be mad," said Ash. "But I really am sorry. And I want the best for you—truly, I do."

All this honesty from Ash was new.

It was like he'd gained a shade of humility. A genuine interest. And it was working Swift in a new way.

It was stripping him of ammunition, of all the sharp things he wanted to say and feel.

"Look—when Edric came over this morning," said Ash, "he was fuming. He laid into me. Said it was me all along who'd been a terrible friend. Pointed out how jealous of you I am. Said that if it weren't for you, I'd have died in the water. Told me lots of other things I'd like not to repeat."

Swift recognized a familiar mortification in Ash's voice. Edric could be very mean, and he would've had no problem laying into Ash. There's no telling how far he took this.

"Don't listen too keenly to Edric," said Swift. "He can be a beast when he's angry. He says and does things that he later regrets."

"He didn't say or do anything I didn't deserve. I've given Edric back all your books. Or—I soon will. They're all boxed up for him to collect."

All Swift's books about sea legends and treasure...

But Swift couldn't stomach the thought of those books. He couldn't even think about the Star of Atlantis without seeing Caius bloodless on the beach; without feeling the hollowness in his heart from believing that Caius had died. From fearing that he might still die.

"Frankly, I don't care about those books." Swift tightened his hand around the Sunstone. "I don't even care about the Star of Atlantis."

"You found it, didn't you?"

Swift glanced at Caius, lying in a dead stillness across the ship. "I wish I hadn't."

"But of course you found it," said Ash. "What is it?"

Swift held the crystal to the sparkling waves and watched their blue shimmer. "A reminder." He lowered it. "I can't believe I was stupid enough not to see that this chase could kill us."

"You couldn't have known," said Ash.

"You seemed to know."

"I was only playing games with you. I pretended to set out when you did, just to drive you mad. To make you waste your time. I knew this was the last weekend you could've gone after the Star of Atlantis."

"Well I'm finished playing games," said Swift.

"I am too," said Ash. "The next time there's something interesting to find—why don't we think about going together?"

That was exactly the vision Caius had tried to give Swift. He wanted Swift and Ash to get over their petty war and revive the true friendship they'd once had.

Swift studied the Sunstone. "I don't think I still have it in me to care about treasures and legends."

"Don't say that," said Ash. "I know you don't mean it. You were burning to know what was in the chest I found. Aren't you still curious?"

"Would you even tell me?" asked Swift. "You didn't want to before."

"Things have changed," said Ash. "And anyway, you found the Star of Atlantis, so there's no point in me hiding what I found."

"Is it really related to the Star of Atlantis?"

"Well—yes and no," said Ash. "It was papers. Old papers. That's all. They seem to be records of daily life—boring things like growing crops and fishing and the weather. But if you ask me, I wonder whether there isn't more to them."

"What makes you think that there's more?"

"I don't exactly know. It's just—who would put fishing and harvesting logs in a chest and then hide it in a waterproof, weatherproof cavern? The museum curator who's keeping the chest is pretty knowledgeable about Celtic history. He believes the papers were created and hidden by a Welsh clan, long ago— a clan that sought to protect things, like treasures. Including the Star of Atlantis."

A clan of treasure protectors.

The chest might've belonged to the same Celtic people who

created the block print of Sterncastle Cove—the Shepherds of the Stars.

"I think I know of that clan." Swift pushed to an elbow.

But a wallop of pain to the chest dropped him back to lying down.

"I'm not surprised that you would," said Ash. "Your research of the Star of Atlantis had to be incredible."

"So—when you said your find was a lead to the Star of Atlantis—"

"That was only a hope," said Ash. "Or I guess it might be more on point to say it was a lie. Something that I wanted to be true. To be honest—I still hope it's true, and it might be. There's a seven-pointed Celtic star fastened inside of the chest. It's just like what's referenced in Star of Atlantis lore. Why couldn't that be a clue that the two are related?"

It wasn't a bad theory, though it was loose. Swift found himself hoping, with Ash, that it was true.

"I'd love for you to take a look at the chest," said Ash, "at its notes. Maybe you could spot something we've missed."

The idea of getting to see what was in that treasure chest felt like a win. And the thought of doing it together with Ash felt good.

As much as it surprised him, Swift was finding that he wanted Ash close again. But he always had, deep down. He'd just let go of the hope that it ever could happen.

Swift glanced at Caius, sleeping. Caius, ever hopeful.

"I have the Practicum trials waiting," said Swift. "I won't have time any longer for treasures and legends."

"Maybe you'll find time," said Ash. "But if not, you'll be brilliant at the Practicum competition. I know you will."

A sharp strike of pain raced up Swift's chest. It was like he'd moved carelessly and brushed the cut—but he was lying perfectly still.

"I don't know. Caius was going to..."

The medic in the blue scrubs was now leaning over Caius. He seemed to be examining him. And then injecting medicine through an IV.

With the blanket thrown off, Caius didn't look like himself.

He looked thinner. And grayer. Like the sun shining down couldn't touch him.

"Caius was going to help me prepare for the exams," said Swift, "Now, he's—"

"—I know what a dangerous place Caius is in," said Ash. "But the medic said he's going to be all right. I know that you're badly hurt, too. And Swift, the resentment I've always felt for you, the need to see you fail—it's gone. If you want me around as you go for that Practicum, I'd really like to be there."

There was an appeal to the thought of Ash—the old Ash— around. The old Ash cheering him on.

"Maybe I could help you study or something," said Ash.

Swift let out a small laugh that the cut, searing, ended. "School's never been your thing."

"Right," said Ash. "I probably couldn't help much. But I do want to support you. You see, when Edric described what happened to you—the danger you were in—I think I understood what you might've felt all those years ago, with me under the water. I know it now—you didn't want me to die."

"If you'd drowned that day," said Swift, "a part of me would've died."

"Well a part of me has died. Please believe me—I'd do anything to help you."

The thought of Ash by his side was a thrill that Swift never imagined he'd feel again. The vision of it seemed as healing as the pain medicine running through him.

"I believe you," said Swift.

Ash was quiet a minute, and then—"So, how do we come back from where we've been?"

"I guess," said Swift, "we just come back." He held tighter the Sunstone. Felt of its clever rhombus outline and sharp corners. "You're going to lose it when you see the Star of Atlantis."

"Is it something valuable?"

"I don't know if it's worth any money. But it's marvelous."

The pain medicine in the IV seemed to be wearing off, and breathing was triggering a deep ache.

"It's a Sunstone," said Swift. "An ancient device that—"

"—that guides lost sailors—I know about those! I've read about them."

The excitement in Ash's voice was timeless. This was the fun exhilaration Swift remembered loving about him.

"Where have you read about them?" Swift managed.

"Hey, when you get home, would you like me to teach you how to handle a treasure find? You might want to get in touch with my contact, at the Welsh museum, to have your discovery documented."

Ash's words seemed to be running together, twisting inside a dizziness striking. Swift tried to sit up some, to focus, but it felt like he was dropping under the water, his body churning in powerful waves.

"When you come back home, would you like me to introduce you to the museum curator?" asked Ash.

"Yes..." Swift could barely get the word out. "But..."

"Hey—you okay? It sounds like you're in a lot of pain—like you just took a punch to the stomach or something."

Swift clenched the mattress to manage the feeling of sinking.

The deepness of the pain brought to mind the grave look that visited the medic when he bathed Swift's cut; the fearful expression on the Scottish sailor when he opened Swift's shirt.

The truth was—Swift might not come back home.

"This cut, Ash. It's bad." Swift spent a moment just breathing, gathering strength to speak. "I searched for help. I found a fisherman. I startled him. He cut me."

"Hang on—the medic told me you fell on some beach rubbish."

"The fisherman," Swift managed. "The things he said were wild. It was like he was a treasure protector. He knew about the Star of Atlantis—more than what books can tell. The medic doesn't believe me."

"Why wouldn't he believe you?"

"He thinks I dreamed it all. Or hallucinated. But I didn't, Ash. I couldn't have."

"On this score, maybe I can help you," said Ash. "I'll see what else I can find about that clan of treasure protectors."

Swift twisted to his side, the pain blinding him. "And the Sunstone—Ash, if I don't come home..."

"Hey, you're scaring me," said Ash. "Of course you're coming home. Say it to me, all right? Say you know it."

This was Ash pressing Swift in his persuasive way, to shape the world the way that he wanted it.

Swift wished he could say it, if for no other reason than to comfort Ash.

But he could no longer say anything. The pain of the cut was a fierce burn now, and he could scarcely do more than breathe. He could scarcely breathe.

He reached for the bed rail and pushed a red button.

The medic, along with the nurse, hurried in. The nurse took the phone from him while the medic laid him out on his back.

He couldn't help the scream that came.

The medic loaded another syringe and fed it into his IV.

"He's in a bad place, with lots of pain," said the nurse, quietly, to Ash. "But we'll do all we can."

Swift tried to catch the nurse's glance. "Tell him—"

The medic pulled the gauze away from Swift's chest. "Don't try to speak, now. I've given you something strong for the pain. I'm also going to give you something to make you sleep, so we can properly tend this cut."

"Wait." Swift stared at the nurse, speaking to Ash. "Tell him," he forced, "come to Bristol."

"He'd like for you to come to Bristol," said the nurse. "Can I say that you will?" She met Swift's stare and nodded.

"You're going to drop well asleep in a moment, nice and comfortable." The medic flicked bubbles out of a syringe.

But—if he slept, he might never see Caius again. If he slept, he might never wake up.

Swift pushed away the medic's hands.

"There, lad." The medic dabbed tears off Swift's cheeks. "You're going to be all right, and so is your brother."

Swift slackened his grip on the medic's arm.

"That's right." The medic connected the syringe to Swift's IV. "You'll be off dreaming in ten...nine...eight..."

"Don't cry, lad," said the nurse. "Your friend will be well cared for—that, I can promise you. The best way you can help Swift is to see that your father finds his parents as quickly as possible."

"Seven...six..."

"The sooner they can make it to Bristol"—the nurse gazed at Swift—"the better."

THE END

READ THE STAR OF ATLANTIS SERIES!

ALSO BY TRICIA D. WAGNER

WHAT MANNER OF LEGENDS MIGHT DARKNESS CONCEAL?

*"**SUN CHILD OF THE MOOR** IS A WELL-WRITTEN, BEAUTIFULLY POETIC, FANTASTICAL TALE, EXPERTLY BLENDING MAGIC WITH REALITY. SYLPHIC FOLKLORE IS UNIQUE TO THIS BOOK AND HOLDS THE POWER OF BELIEVABILITY THANKS TO WAGNER'S MASTERFUL WRITING. THE FAMILIAL INTERACTIONS ARE REMINISCENT OF **A WRINKLE IN TIME**, MAKING IT A DELIGHTFULLY IMMERSIVE TALE OF LOVE AND PERSONAL GROWTH, WELL SUITED TO YOUNG AND ADULT READERS WHO ENJOY EXPLORING THE WORLD'S UNLIMITED POSSIBILITIES THROUGH A MAGICAL LENS."*
-MARY R. LANNI, MLIS, *REEDSY DISCOVERY*

*"**SUN CHILD OF THE MOOR**, WITH ITS LIVELY, ENGAGING ACTION WILL ENCOURAGE DISCUSSION AND DEBATE IN READER CIRCLES ABOUT THE CONSEQUENCES OF SPECIAL ABILITIES AND THE CONTRAST BETWEEN IMAGINATION AND REALITY, MAKING THIS BOOK A TOP RECOMMENDATION ABOVE MANY OTHER ACTION-PACKED FANTASIES."*
-D. DONOVAN, SR. REVIEWER, *MIDWEST BOOK REVIEW*

FREE EBOOK

Night Swiftly Falling
by Tricia D. Wagner

Eight-year-old Swift is lost in dreams of sea legends and pirate adventures, until an encounter with the deadly power of the ocean shocks him into reality. Swift struggles to hang onto his childhood fantasies, but his new understanding of the fragile nature of life and friendships threatens to swamp his hope.
Under the guidance of his older brother, Caius, Swift must learn to brave the challenging waves of change without losing himself to their destruction.

To get your FREE eBook, visit:
Night Swiftly Falling

ABOUT THE AUTHOR

Tricia D. Wagner is an award-winning novelist, poet, and short story writer. She grew up in Amarillo, Texas, chasing storms, riding stallions, sojourning through painted canyons, disappearing into floating mesas under starry skies.

She now lives in Rockford, Illinois (though the truth is, she's a citizen of a dozen fictional countries). Tricia works in research and lives day to day wonderstruck but luckily can feel her way about this terrifying, beautiful Earth through writing.

Tricia has pieces published in the *Write City Magazine*, *Chicago Newa*, *Word of Art 3D*, *Literary Yard*, and *Midwest Review*.

To learn more about Tricia, sign up for her readers' club, and hear about upcoming releases, visit:

www.TriciaWagner.com

AUTHOR'S NOTE

I love connecting with readers and writers. If, you're interested in stories, then you're a kindred spirit to me, and I have lots more in store for you. To quote another kindred spirit in writing, Jedi Master Stephen King:

"Writing is magic, as much as the water of life as any other art. The water is free. So drink. Drink and be filled up."

If you're interested not only in stories, but in story creation, visit my website and sign up to receive a FREE **'Story Kickoff Character Worksheet.'**

I designed this tool for that first moment of getting our feet wet at the brink of a story.

To get your free worksheet, visit:
www.TriciaWagner.com